W9-CXQ-631

Neither of the goons said a thing as they took the elevator up to the penthouse. Both of them were very large men, at least six-four and 250 pounds.

"It must be a real interesting job," Carter said to them as they were riding up.

One of them looked at him but said nothing.

"I mean, traveling around the world with Rojas, seeing all those gorgeous women, seeing all the booze and the gambling . . . and not being able to touch one bit of it."

"Shut up, or I will break your arm," one of them said.

Carter chuckled. "Anytime you'd like to try it, pal, just say the word."

NICK CARTER IS IT!

"Nick Carter out-Bonds James Bond."
—*Buffalo Evening News*

"Nick Carter is America's #1 espionage agent."
—*Variety*

"Nick Carter is razor-sharp suspense."
—*King Features*

"Nick Carter is extraordinarily big."
—*Bestsellers*

"Nick Carter has attracted an army of addicted readers
. . . the books are fast, have plenty of action and just the
right degree of sex . . . Nick Carter is the American
James Bond, suave, sophisticated, a killer with both the
ladies and the enemy."
—*The New York Times*

FROM THE NICK CARTER KILLMASTER SERIES

NICK CARTER

KILLMASTER

Death Hand Play

C

CHARTER BOOKS, NEW YORK

''Nick Carter'' is a registered trademark of The Condé Nast
Publications, Inc., registered in the United States Patent Office.

All characters in this book are fictitious.
Any resemblance to actual persons, living or dead,
is purely coincidental.

DEATH HAND PLAY

A Charter Book/published by arrangement with
The Condé Nast Publications, Inc.

PRINTING HISTORY
Charter Original/September 1984

All rights reserved.
Copyright © 1984 by The Condé Nast Publications, Inc.
This book may not be reproduced in whole
or in part, by mimeograph or any other means,
without permission. For information address:
The Berkley Publishing Group, 200 Madison Avenue,
New York, New York 10016

ISBN: 0-441-14222-2

Charter Books are published by The Berkley Publishing Group,
200 Madison Avenue, New York, N.Y. 10016
PRINTED IN THE UNITED STATES OF AMERICA

*Dedicated to the men of the
Secret Services of the United
States of America*

PROLOGUE

Patrick Foster, Central Intelligence Agency liaison officer with the British Secret Intelligence Service, stepped out of the front doors of the U.S. embassy on Grosvenor Square in London and sniffed the damp night air. It smelled of automobile exhaust, of the Thames, and of that something else that all big cities have in common.

It was nearly ten in the evening, and Foster was tired. It had been a long day. The Russians were at it again; at least three new Aeroflot employees, just flown in, were almost certainly KGB agents.

On top of all that, Major Carey Harrell, his old friend from the SIS, had telephoned that Juan Rojas was in town, and probably up to no good.

Rojas was a name long known to Foster, who before his London assignment had been stationed at the consulate in Rio de Janeiro. Rojas was a fabulously wealthy Brazilian who owned tens of thousands of acres of farmland and timberland, two newspapers, an asbestos mine, and a significant portion of Rio's magnificent waterfront.

As rich as Rojas was, he was equally anti-American. It was said, but not yet proven, that Rojas had many connections with Cuba and with Libya. He had been seen on more than one occasion meeting with PLO leader Yasir Arafat. And he was considered *persona non grata* in a number of countries, including, of course, Israel.

It was suspected that the tall, handsome, suave, and very sophisticated Rojas had been involved in a number of schemes to hurt or at least to embarrass the U.S. government.

In all likelihood, a number of his subsidiary companies had been at work for years in an attempt to manipulate the American stock market. He had been linked to at least three major counterfeiting rings. He had been tied to organized crime as well as to drug connections between Colombia and Florida's Gulf Coast.

Whenever Rojas moved, the United States was very interested.

In the back courtyard of the embassy, Foster climbed into his Ford Cortina, then drove around to the front and was let out the main gate, where he merged smoothly with the Friday night traffic.

Foster was a short man, thin but wiry, with a terrier's face. He had been born and raised in Brooklyn, and had been a tough, streetwise kid. He was no different now. He had the big-city savvy, but it was tempered with the sophistication that comes with doing a difficult job in a variety of locations.

He lit a cigarette as he drove to his rendezvous with Harrell. Rojas had apparently entered the country sometime that morning. His passport had been flagged, and in due course the information had gotten over to the SIS offices in Whitehall.

The South American had checked into a suite at the Ritz on Piccadilly. There he had rested, then had had a couple of drinks at the bar before going out for the evening.

He was currently at the Alhambra, London's poshest private gambling establishment. Harrell and another SIS legman were stationed nearby, watching. They had telephoned Foster and invited him along.

"After all, he is your show, even if he's on our turf at the moment," Harrell had said brightly.

Foster promised he'd be right there, but Harrell had assured him that Rojas probably wouldn't be moving from the club until well after two in the morning.

"These things often go all night, you know," the SIS man had said.

Before Foster had left the embassy, he had pulled out Rojas's folder, then had called up the computer at Langley via their real-time satellite link for more information.

The data had still been coming over when he had finally left. But he had annotated the file as well as the station log that he was going out with Harrell and an SIS stakeout team to see what Rojas might be up to.

Cover your ass. At all costs, cover your ass. Don't put yourself out on a limb no matter how busy or distracted you might be. It was axiomatic. And he had complied, although he didn't think much would come of this.

Rojas probably just breezed into London for a little gambling. When he was done, he'd be off to another world capital somewhere, giving some other case officer heartburn.

But in the meantime, he was Foster's headache.

The Alhambra was well out on Whitechapel Road, and it took Foster forty-five minutes to make it to where his SIS friend was parked in a Volkswagen minibus, its windows covered with reflective screens.

He circled the area twice, cruising slowly past the van, which had been parked half a block from the ornate front entrance to the exclusive club.

A constant stream of luxury automobiles came and went, pausing a moment at the front doors of the club to either take on or discharge their beautifully dressed passengers. Rolls-Royces, big Mercedeses, Bentleys, and Jaguars gleamed under the streetlights.

Foster finally pulled up behind the VW and killed his lights. He sat there for several seconds, the motor softly ticking over, until he shut off the ignition and climbed out.

Harrell got out the back door of the van and came over to Foster.

"Patrick—so glad you could join us for this little party," he said. They shook hands. They could just see the Alhambra's entrance from where they stood hidden by the van.

"Anything interesting happening?"

Harrell shook his head. "Nothing yet. But I didn't expect anything much different." He glanced again toward the club. "We tracked him from the Ritz around eight, as I told you on the phone. He's been inside ever since."

"No back doors?"

"Two. I've got a man on each."

A Mercedes rolled slowly by, its powerful headlights illuminating them as if they were onstage under spotlights. Then it slid past and pulled up to the front of the club.

"Inside," Harrell said.

He and Foster climbed into the van. A third man, in shirt sleeves, was hunched over a set of very powerful-looking binoculars trained out the windshield toward the front entrance.

"Pat Foster, this is Lieutenant Floyd Chamberlain."

Chamberlain looked up from the binoculars and nodded. He and Foster shook hands, and the Englishman moved aside.

"Care for a look-see, sir?"

"Sure," Foster said.

Through the windshield, without the binoculars, the club

entrance was just a well-lit blur. Foster could see people and movement, but not in any detail.

He hunched down behind the binoculars and looked through the lenses. The entrance to the building leaped up at him in startling detail and clarity. He could see that the screws holding the license plate into its holder on the back of the Mercedes were of the normal, slotted type. And he could see that the man was wearing formal pumps, one of the bows bent over.

"Nice," he said, and he whistled.

"Rather," Chamberlain agreed.

Foster looked up. "He went in, but he hasn't come out?"

"Just so, sir," Chamberlain said. He reached over and flipped on a radio. "One," he said softly.

"Yes?"

"Anything?"

"Negative."

"Two?" Chamberlain said into the microphone.

There was no response.

Harrell, who had been staring out the windshield toward the club, looked back.

"Two?" Chamberlain repeated.

Still there was no answer.

Chamberlain looked up at Harrell, who grabbed the microphone. "One," he said.

"Yes?"

"Nothing out of two. Pop 'round and check."

"Right-o."

"Probably just equipment trouble, sir," Chamberlain said.

Foster lit a cigarette after first offering the pack. Both of the other men declined.

Several cars slid up to the club to let off passengers, and

still there was nothing. Harrell keyed the mike again.

"One," he said.

There was nothing.

"One," he said a little more urgently. "One or two—come in, please."

"Bloody hell," Chamberlain muttered after a moment. He climbed forward and got behind the wheel of the van. In seconds he had the engine started and they were racing down the block, around the corner, and finally around the second corner, behind the club.

"There," Harrell said softly, pointing toward a Vauxhall parked half up on the curb. Harrell had his gun out as Chamberlain drove past. There were two men in the front seat of the car.

Foster didn't like this at all. Something big was going down. He pulled out his .38 Police Special as Chamberlain stood on the brakes.

All three of them were out of the van and racing back to the small car, when the car doors opened and the two men jumped out.

"Aubrey?" Harrell called.

Too late Foster realized what was happening, and he never had a chance to raise his weapon. "Aw, shit . . ." he said as both men from the little car dropped into the classic shooter's stance and opened fire. He never felt a thing. The last thing he was aware of was Harrell and Chamberlain going down on either side of him, blood spraying everywhere.

ONE

Nick Carter was not overly tall, perhaps a little over six feet. He was very well built and seemed athletic in a rugged sort of way. He was slightly graying at the temples, and had craggy features and deep, silent dark eyes that at times could be very hard. But there was a bit of humanity in the lines around the corners of his mouth and eyes. His was the face that had seen a lot and would probably see more.

He was a professional and very good at his job, which lent him an air of confidence that was unmistakable to even the most casual observer.

It was early on a Saturday morning, before eight, when he emerged from his Arlington condo, got into his gunmetal gray E-type Jaguar, and headed across the Potomac toward Dupont Circle.

It was early fall, and Washington, D.C., was in full session after the summer recess. There had been a cocktail party at the Salvadoran embassy on California Avenue the night before, one of several Carter had attended in the last couple of weeks as per a State Department request. Carter, along with a number of Central Intelligence Agency spooks and a few knowledgeable old hands from the FBI, had been asked to cover the opening rounds of parties as the season got into full swing.

Dimitri Romanov, the KGB *rezident* here in Washington, was up to something. It was a sort of all-hands alert—at least for the moment.

Carter, who worked for AXE, the most supersecret intelligence agency in the free world, had been languishing at headquarters on Dupont Circle for want of an assignment for six months. Even the embassy "binge-and-barf circuit," as it was so picturesquely called, was better than nothing. Except that it raised hell with his physical conditioning regimen.

Carter was a case officer, a field man. One of the best AXE had ever seen. For some years he had been a member of an elite group of men with a license to kill in the course of carrying out their assignments. His designation was N3. A Killmaster. And he was good. Very good.

He turned on the radio and lit one of his very strong, custom-blended cigarettes as he drove.

The Jaguar was his latest acquisition. He had flown out to California six weeks earlier to purchase the vehicle, and he had driven it back from L.A. nonstop in a little over forty-eight hours. It wasn't something he had to do, nor was fast driving a compulsion with him. AXE's doctors called him a "hard-charger" for want of a better description. He was a man with a very high degree of survival instinct and with a very low tolerance for boredom. A very dangerous combination.

He punched the Jag into second gear and stood on the accelerator, the RPM needle winding out around six grand, then slipped it into third, the car shooting around the long curve toward P Street.

An hour and a half ago, he had been awakened out of a fitful sleep by the telephone. It was David Hawk himself. The sun had just come up, and the top-floor apartment was bathed in a golden glow.

"Nicholas?" Hawk's gruff voice came over the line.

Carter was instantly awake. There were very few men that Carter totally respected. David Hawk, AXE's hard-bitten chief, was at the top of that very short list. Over the years, Carter and the ex-OSS man had developed a very close relationship; it was almost that of father and son, minus most of the outward trappings of affection.

They were two men who had each other's measure. Each respected the other. One was a professional; the other, older and wiser, was a professional's professional.

"Good morning, sir," Carter said. He looked over at the clock radio as the pretty Salvadoran stirred in her sleep. The sheet had slipped off her shoulder, exposing her left breast. Her skin was soft and tawny, the areola and nipple of her breast a dark brown, almost black.

"How are you feeling?"

"This morning, sir, or in general?" Carter asked, suddenly very alert. Hawk only opened a conversation like that when he wanted to propose a particularly tough assignment.

"Both."

"Fit, sir. Very fit."

"We'll see."

"Sir?"

"I want you over here by . . . eight. The others are on their way."

The others would be there. The entire team. Armorer. Backgrounds. Archives. Coordination. It was an assignment.

"I can be there in half an hour, sir—" Carter started to say, but Hawk cut him off.

"Er, I believe you have an obligation to take care of first . . ."

Carter looked down at the girl. Her name was Maria Ines.

He remembered it from the name tag she wore on her very low-cut cocktail dress. It was off the shoulder and a vivid pink.

"Yes, sir," he said. The girl was now awake. She was looking up at him with very large, dark brown eyes.

"Eight o'clock will be sufficient. I don't want any suspicions centered around you just at this moment."

"Is that an order, sir?" Carter asked delicately.

For a moment there was silence on the line, then Hawk laughed out loud. "An order," he managed. "Yes, Nick, I'll see you at eight."

"Yes, sir," Carter said, and he hung up the telephone. Maria Ines was smiling.

"You have to attend to something this morning?" she asked innocently. Almost certainly she was with her government's small but reasonably effective military intelligence service.

Carter nodded. "That was my boss with my orders."

"Yes?" the girl said, her eyes shining.

"He knows you're here."

She said nothing. But a wary expression had crept into her eyes.

"He told me that no matter what happened this morning, I was to attend to you."

"What does that mean?"

Slowly Carter pulled the sheet back, revealing her other lovely breast, her slightly rounded stomach, the very dark tuft of pubic hair, and her long, beautifully formed legs.

"What do you think it means?" Carter asked seriously.

"I don't know," the girl replied. She was somewhat uneasy.

There were a number of old scars on Carter's body. At least three of them were obviously gunshot wounds. Inevitably when he made love with a woman for the first time she was drawn to the scars, fascinated by what they meant. But very few came out and asked him about them. But they did color his relationships. It was no different now with Maria Ines. She was at once fascinated and frightened by Carter, especially since he was now being so deliberately mysterious.

He reached out and caressed the nipples of her breasts with his fingertips, then trailed upward to her long, slender neck, where he lingered for a moment.

She licked her lips, her mouth half parted. It was obvious she wanted to be excited, but she was nervous.

"You seem to be frightened of something," Carter said. "Of me?"

She touched his cheek with her long fingernails. "Who are you?" she asked softly. "Why were you at the party last night? Who invited you?"

Carter smiled, not unkindly. "If I told you the State Department, would you believe me?"

She shrugged, her right leg coming up. Her nipples were erect. Carter could feel himself responding. "I might. But it still doesn't answer my question."

"I was sent to seduce you," Carter said.

"Really?" she said. She was frightened again, but she was trying to hide it. She seemed at that moment like a doe in the deep forest who had never seen a man before but somehow knew this one was very dangerous.

Carter leaned forward and kissed her breasts, circling the nipples with his tongue. She arched her back, a slight groan of pleasure escaping from her sensuous lips.

He raised his head and looked into her eyes. "My boss thinks you are here to spy on us."

"What do you think?" she asked. She was already starting to breathe hard. Last night she had been a tigress, proving there *was* something to the Latin-lover myth after all. And it applied equally well to women. . . .

It was his turn to shrug. He bent down again, this time trailing his tongue from the nipples of her breasts downward to her stomach and her navel.

"*Madre*," she breathed. "You did not answer me."

Again Carter lifted himself up so that he could look at her. Her lips were moist; her breasts rose and fell. She was beginning to pant.

"I don't give a damn if you are or you aren't. You didn't get anything from me, because I don't have anything worth telling."

"What about your report?"

He caressed the tops of her legs, then the insides of her thighs as she automatically opened up for him. "There will be no report. What would I say—that we made love?"

She laughed deep in her throat, but that changed to a deep, primal moan of pleasure as Carter bent down, his head between her legs, his hands on the taut rounds of her buttocks, and he parted her soft folds with his tongue.

Soon she was moving almost uncontrollably, pressing his head to her with her hands, and then her back was arched high, her heels dug into the mattress, and she stifled a long, low scream that slowly subsided, her body in such fine tune now that the slightest movement from Carter caused her to jerk as if she were shot with a gun.

When he finally pulled himself away and looked down at her, her eyes were wild, her lips parted.

She pushed him over onto his back, and she was on him, taking him into her mouth, while her fingers caressed every part of his body that she could reach.

Carter smiled as he braked to a halt at P Street, then turned right and drove the last few blocks to Dupont Circle. He had had the devil's own time getting rid of her in time to take a quick shower, jump into a pullover sweater, slacks, and a pair of soft, slip-on boots, and getting out of there himself.

When she got back to her embassy she would be very embarrassed to find out that Carter had discovered the tiny tape recorder in her purse and had erased everything. She would be hard pressed to explain what she had done with her night. In any event, Carter figured she wouldn't last too long in her present job. Using sex to gain an intelligence goal was as old a technique as the very act of spying. But the technique did not work if the agent was so passionate she forgot what she was supposed to be doing. Maria Ines was such a woman. She had a lot of sensuality . . . too much for the job she was trying to do.

AXE was housed in the Amalgamated Press and Wire Services Building on Dupont Circle. As far as intelligence agencies the world over went, it was fairly small. It did have offices—under the guise of the wire service—in many foreign cities, but its budget was nowhere near the CIA's or the KGB's. But AXE was highly effective. The dirtiest, messiest situations were grist for Hawk's mill. A job the CIA or the National Security Agency would not or could not do, AXE took on.

For Nick Carter to be called in, something like that was apparently brewing.

His identification was checked at the entrance to the sub-basement garage, and he parked his car in his private slot, then went up in the elevator to his little office in Operations.

Only the weekend OD and his two runners were on duty in Operations as Carter crossed the long, fluorescent-lit room, flipped on the lights to his office, checked his recorder for incoming messages, and lit another cigarette.

There was nothing of consequence on the machine: a couple of bitches from housekeeping about his misuse of the AXE safe house in Athens—but that complaint was nearly a year old—and one question about some expense account item of eight months ago.

Back out in the Operations room, the OD looked up. "Mr. Hawk would like you to go right up, sir."

"Thanks," Carter said, crossing to the back and taking the restricted access elevator up to Hawk's office. He had to sign in with security before he was allowed through the heavy steel doors into the main corridor.

Hawk's secretary, Ginger Bateman, was not there, but the inner door was open. Spasso Kerchefski, AXE's eccentric but brilliant armorer, came to the door. "He's here. Come in, Carter. We're waiting."

David Hawk, a short, tough-looking, craggy-faced man with a thick shock of white hair and the inevitable cheap cigar clenched in his teeth, sat behind his littered desk. His jacket was off, his tie loose, his shirt sleeves rolled up. He had almost certainly been there most of the night if not all of it, Carter thought.

Hawk looked up. "I trust you took care of everything with the girl, N3?"

"Yes, sir," Carter said. Kerchefski was the only member of the AXE team there with Hawk.

"That will be all, Mr. Kerchefski," Hawk said.

"Shall I remain on call?"

"Yes. We may need you a little later this morning."

"Of course," the bushy-eyebrowed armorer said, and he left, quietly closing the office door behind him. A green light came on over the door, indicating that the room's automatic debugging and sweeping devices had discovered nothing. In the parlance, they were "clean."

"Have a seat, Nick," Hawk said. "No complications this morning?"

"None, sir. I'll dictate a report."

Hawk nodded. He relit his cigar, apparently giving himself

time to think out just how he was going to put whatever it was he had to say to Carter.

Carter knew his boss well enough to understand this gesture as well. When Hawk stalled for even a second of time, something very unusual and difficult was in the offing. Carter took a deep breath, forcing himself to calm down. He wanted out of the humdrum routine of Washington in the worst way.

"Does the name Juan Rojas mean anything to you?" Hawk asked, sitting back.

Carter searched his memory, but the name meant nothing to him. "No, sir. Afraid not."

"He's not exactly a household word in this country, although in Brazil and a few other places he's either a saint or the devil, depending upon who you talk to."

"I see."

Hawk opened a thick file folder, pulled out a few glossy eight-by-tens, and handed them across. "Rojas," he said.

The first showed a man dressed in a tuxedo in a group of men and women about to get into some kind of a luxury bus. He was tall, well built, and good-looking in a dark, Latin way. The second showed a man in swimming trunks beside a pool. There were a half-dozen other men, and at least a dozen women, at poolside; all the women were beautiful, all of them nude. The third showed Rojas from an overhead camera. He was seated at a baccarat table in some casino. He had a seven and a king, and had apparently just drawn another card. It was a two, making a perfect nine.

Carter looked up.

"The first is outside his office in Rio de Janeiro. The second was taken at his home outside the city, and the third—Monte Carlo."

"He is a very lucky man at gambling," Carter said.

"Rojas is very lucky at everything he does, N3. But he has a lot of help with his luck, if you get my meaning."

"Does he cheat at cards?"

Hawk smiled. "Wouldn't we all if we could get away with it?" he asked rhetorically. "The man was fabulously wealthy by any standard. His fortune was estimated, four years ago, at somewhere in the neighborhood of five hundred million dollars."

"*Was* wealthy, sir?"

"From what we can gather. Senhor Rojas has been having some trouble lately. One of his mines suffered a series of disasters—that was in September. His newspapers were struck. Terrorists have blown up his television studios, and the world money market has not been kind to his investments in the last quarter."

"Have we had anything to do with any of that, sir?"

"AXE hasn't. At least directly. The CIA has a few people in Geneva, and the Israelis seem to have managed some of the messier operations."

"Why are they picking on this guy?"

"He's a friend of Arafat and of Colonel Kaddafi. The Israelis have even contemplated assassination or kidnapping, but they were talked out of it."

Now Hawk was getting to it, Carter guessed.

Hawk opened the file folder and consulted a couple of documents. "You'll get this file this morning, and you'll have plenty of time to look it over. To make a long story short, Rojas has been conclusively linked with Soviet intelligence. From what we understand, he's promised the Russians he could deliver the Caribbean basin to them on a silver platter. He's been helped in certain areas during the last few years, but now, ever since Grenada, things have changed. The documents we found there were damned embarrassing to the Cubans as well as to the Russians."

"You think the Russians are calling in their chit?" Carter asked.

"That's exactly what we thought a couple of months ago," Hawk said, glancing again at some of the pages in the file. He closed the cover and handed the bulky folder across to Carter. "You can pull up the Company's info on the computer after we're done here." Hawk looked at his watch. "You have a few hours yet before your London plane leaves."

"London?"

"Yes. I haven't finished bringing you up-to-date yet."

"No, sir."

"Rojas is planning something; we're fairly certain of it. A KGB agent has met with him on three occasions that we know of. The pressure is on. Deliver or else."

"What can he do? I mean with his fortune either mostly gone or dried up, what's left for him?"

"Don't underestimate this man, Nick. He may no longer have control of a half billion in cash, but the power and influence the man wields is enormous."

"I don't understand."

"He's not exactly destitute—at least not yet. No hotel in the world would turn him away. His credit is good in any room of any casino in the world."

"That's all well and good, sir, but—"

"The man has the power to make waves, very large waves. If he decided to publicly announce that he was going to buy Anaconda Copper, there'd be a rush on the stock, which would, of course, immediately go up."

"But just temporarily, until it was discovered he had nothing with which to back his announcement."

"That doesn't matter. By then the harm would be done."

"He's planning something for the Caribbean? A revolution? Something coordinated with Castro, no doubt. Perhaps even through drug connections . . . I assume he's been into that?"

Hawk nodded. "The President's war on drugs in Florida was mostly aimed at Rojas's operations."

"And were we effective?"

"Very."

"Why are we still worried about Rojas's adventures in the area?"

"Until last night," Hawk said, "we had begun to think that Rojas was dormant. We now think our previous speculations were wrong."

It was like a telescope. The focus was becoming finer by the second.

"A Company man by the name of Patrick Foster, trade mission with our embassy in London, along with four SIS men—among them, Carey Harrell—was on a routine surveillance last night of Rojas, who had entered the country that morning. They traced him to a suite at the Ritz, and later that evening the man went gambling at some fancy club outside of the city."

Something was coming. Carter could feel it.

"While Rojas was in the club, Foster, Harrell, and the three others were gunned down in the street."

"Who did it?"

Hawk smiled wanly and shook his head. "It was made to appear that two of the SIS men had been turned, and shot it out with Foster, Harrell, and another fellow named Chamberlain."

"And Chamberlain or one of the others, before he died, just managed to kill the other two."

Hawk nodded. "Rojas is up to something. We want to know what. And we want to stop it, of course."

"Why us, sir? I would have thought this would be a hot item for the Company. One of their own dead and all."

"The DCI called me personally last night," Hawk said.

"He thinks this is going to be a particularly . . . unique job."

"Sir?"

Hawk sat forward. His cigar had gone out. "Rojas runs in some fairly exclusive circles. In order to find out what he's up to, in order for us to effectively find out why Foster and the others were killed, we're going to have to put someone in the midst of Rojas's world. Someone who can handle himself aboard a yacht or in a drawing room. Someone who knows how to dress . . . who knows how to handle himself with spoiled, pampered, beautiful women. Someone who can gamble. In short, we need a playboy . . . or someone who can pass as a playboy yet is deadly enough to handle himself."

Carter held himself very erect but said nothing.

"The CIA has no one. The SIS might, but they have other troubles. The DCI asked me. You're the man, Nick. You fill the bill perfectly."

TWO

The Supersonic British Airways Concorde, its futuristic nose drooping like some stylized bird of prey's, came in gracefully for a landing at Heathrow Airport. Nick Carter was speedily processed through VIP customs, and literally within minutes of the moment the big plane had touched down, he was climbing into the back seat of a Rolls-Royce Corniche convertible—with the top up, of course—and was being whisked into London.

A uniformed chauffeur drove, the smoked glass partition between the front and back up, and a secretary in a bowler hat sat in the back with Carter.

The car, the driver, and the secretary were all from César Ritz's pile on Piccadilly. From the moment he had arrived at the airport, stateside, Carter had been on his own.

Hawk had assured him that they'd have the complete cooperation of the SIS, at least initially. There were a lot of hard feelings around Whitehall about the fledgling operation, but no one had actually stated his disapproval. Work fast as long as it was on British soil. If Carter failed, or if the situation seemed to be getting out of the ultimate control of the SIS—such as if Rojas suddenly made a dash for one of the

Warsaw Pact countries—then they'd move quickly, agreement or no agreement.

The CIA, of course, had called for AXE's help. They would not interfere.

Most of Carter's wardrobe for this caper had come out of his own closet, although there were a few items from New Bond Street and Savile Row waiting for him in his suite at the Ritz. And Cartier in New York had provided a few accessories, not the least of which was a solid gold cigarette lighter and an ultrathin, hand-hammered gold Vacheron & Constantin dress watch with a band of black water buffalo hide.

AXE's funding section had provided him with a couple of hundred thousand pounds cash, along with a letter of credit on Citicorp for twice that. In his Mark Cross wallet was a gold American Express card, a platinum Diners Club card, and a totally unlimited Carte Blanche card. In addition, memberships at all the clubs had been secured for him.

It seems that Carter's father—of the Carters of Long Island—and two extremely wealthy uncles had all died within the past few years. All three had left their entire estates to Nicholas Carter, who, it was said in certain circles, was supposed to be an absolute marvel at three distinct but related endeavors: playing the American stock market, gambling, and making love.

He wasn't a fighter, but to be blessed with three out of four wasn't bad.

All that was on the plus side. There were some minuses, of course.

AXE's latest intelligence indicated that Rojas had what amounted to practically his own army with him wherever he traveled. If a man could be said to be as impregnable as a fortress, that was Juan Rojas.

Besides his muscle, Rojas was, in the words of AXE Archives, "gun-shy to the limit."

After all, the man had lost a major fortune in the last few years. He was battered. He wasn't going to allow many people to get close enough to hurt him.

Yet that view was hardly consistent with Rojas's gambling in London. That was one of the most foolhardy of all risks. And Rojas, if anything, was certainly not a foolhardy man.

Also on the negative side was the fact that Rojas's people killed a CIA agent and two SIS officers. All professionals. All good men. He was not afraid of overt action. If and when it suited him, he would murder.

The hotel secretary who had been sent out to Heathrow to fetch Carter was a tight-lipped elderly man who had seen kings and queens and billionaires come and go. He was not particularly impressed now, nor was he interested in carrying on a conversation. Had the man been the ordinary, garden-variety hotel employee anywhere else, Carter would have been able, for a fee, to pump the man about the comings and goings of Rojas. Such a suggestion would be unthinkable to this sort, however.

At the hotel, which was near Buckingham Palace, the Royal Academy, St. James's, and almost everything else that was historical or famous in London, Carter made a great show of moving up the grand staircase and crossing the lobby to register.

His ten suitcases came after him, and he followed them up the gold elevator to his suite on one of the top floors overlooking Green Park, St. James's Park, and beyond, the Thames.

The assistant manager and four bellmen, including the bell captain, opened up the room, poured the champagne, unpacked Carter's bags, hung up his clothing, and arranged his cash and credit needs.

When they were finished, Carter passed three hundred pounds to the bell captain to distribute. He had taken the man aside after the assistant manager had left.

"Pop back up here in the next half hour, like a good man," Carter said.

The bell captain, a wily, streetwise man about Carter's age, grinned, showing his teeth. "You'd be interested in a little companionship, sir?" he asked.

"Information," Carter replied.

The man compressed his lips.

"Well-paid-for information."

The bell captain grinned again, and nodded. "Of course, sir. The Ritz is here to serve." He clicked his heels, turned, and breezed out, closing the doors quietly behind him.

Carter waited a minute or so, then he went to the doors and threw them open. The wide corridor was empty. He closed the doors, locked them, and went back inside.

Since the advent of airport security measures, even in VIP processing, Carter had been carrying his weapons in a large radio/cassette recorder that Kerchefski had built for him.

On the bed, he pulled the big radio out of its case, set the proper controls so that the back would open, then eased out the top circuit board.

First out was Wilhelmina, his 9mm Luger, two spare clips of ammunition, and the stubby silencer. He worked the ejector slide several times, loaded the automatic, and levered a round into the chamber. He checked the safety, then laid the weapon aside.

Next came Hugo, his pencil-thin, razor-sharp stiletto with its very plain, leather-wrapped haft. The weapon was silent, deadly, and had gotten him out of more impossible situations than he cared to think about.

Finally came Pierre, a tiny, egg-shaped capsule filled with a deadly and exceedingly fast-acting nerve gas. This, the most sophisticated piece in his arsenal, fit into a pouch high on his inner thigh, very much like a third testicle.

He made sure the doors to his suite were locked from the

inside before he stripped and climbed into the shower, the needle-sharp spray as hot as he could possibly stand it at first. Later he turned off the hot water and steeled himself to remain under an icy blast for a full two minutes.

Afterward, when he had dried himself, he padded back out to his sitting room, put some music on the stereo, poured himself a stiff cognac, and went back into his bedroom. He dressed slowly, strapping his weapons on with care.

Carter was a different sort of person on assignment than when relaxing on vacation or at home. On a job he was almost like an actor, the consummate actor whose audiences had the power of life or death over his performances.

Everything he did out in the field was done with care and with the skill he had learned on hundreds of assignments over the years.

He stopped for a moment to inspect himself in the full-length mirrors on the closet doors. Every assignment brought its own peculiarities, each its own dangers. Carter had developed a sixth sense about such things. At this moment something was telling him to be very careful of Rojas, very careful indeed.

He turned away, sipping his cognac. Rojas was nothing more than a man, once very rich and still very powerful. But there was more. Carter could feel it in the air like some powerful scent.

Back at the mirror he put down his snifter, finished tying his black bow tie, and then he slipped into his tuxedo jacket, adjusting his shoulder holster so that the bulge of his Luger could not be detected—at least not by a nonprofessional.

Carter had just walked back out to his sitting room when the bell captain arrived. He let the man in.

"Good evening, sir. You're looking grand now . . ."

"Thank you, my man," Carter said, smiling. He pulled out his wallet and withdrew a stack of hundred-pound notes.

"Okay, sir," the bell captain said, the obsequiousness gone from his voice, "what is it you want to know?"

"Senhor Juan Rojas."

The bell captain stiffened, but then he smiled. "Of course, sir. What can I tell you?"

Bingo, Carter thought. He had struck a nerve. The man was most likely already on Rojas's payroll. It was interesting to know that Rojas was himself worried about his safety here.

"How long has he been here in the hotel?"

"Do you mean tonight, sir?"

Carter shook his head.

"When did he arrive? Two days ago, sir."

"Where is he at this moment?"

"Downstairs, I believe, in the casino."

"Does he gamble here?"

"Yes, sir. But not very much. Mostly he does his gambling, from what these ears hear, out at the . . ." The bell captain paused as if he had had a lapse of memory. Carter passed him a hundred-pound note. "Oh, yes—it comes to me now. He does most of his gambling out at the Alhambra."

"Where's that?"

The bell captain explained how to get to the place. "Any cabby will know where it is, though."

"Has he been winning?"

"That I couldn't say, sir."

Carter held out another hundred-pound note.

"Sorry, sir, but that one I really can't answer."

Carter nodded and handed him the note anyway. "Is he here alone?"

"Oh, no, sir. Mr. Rojas has quite a contingent with him. Quite a contingent."

"Ladies?"

"Some of them. A lot of bruisers, if you catch my drift. Muscle, you know."

"I see," Carter mused thoughtfully.

"Begging your pardon, sir, but I was just wondering who . . ."

Carter turned away as if he were distracted. He poured himself another cognac. "Yes?" he said.

"It's not often we get guests who ask about other guests. I mean . . ."

Carter waved him off. "Oh, it's nothing illegal, I assure you. I'm here in London for a little action, that's all. I've heard of Rojas. Heard he was quite the gambling man." He grinned. "I intend challenging the fellow. Heard he's well-heeled."

"That he is, sir. That he is indeed. But if you don't mind me saying so, I'd be watching my step if I were you. His muscle doesn't take kindly to anyone prying into Mr. Rojas's private affairs."

"Of course," Carter said. "I think I'll just pop down and pay my respects."

"Up, sir. He's in the penthouse."

"Yes, I'm sure he is. But I thought you said he was in the casino at the moment."

"Oh, yes—indeed he is, sir," the bell captain said. He had pocketed the money. He saluted, turned on his heel, and left.

When he was gone, Carter tossed back his cognac, put the glass aside, then made sure his tie was straight before he pocketed his room key and left.

It was interesting but not surprising that Rojas was here with muscle and that he was surveying his surroundings. But why was he gambling at the Alhambra and apparently no where else? And why, Carter wondered, was he in London gambling at all? It didn't make a lot of sense for a man in his position, a man with a huge IOU due the Soviets.

Carter took the elevator down to the hotel lobby, where he crossed over to the entrance to the casino. He showed his membership card at the door.

It was barely eight o'clock, the dinner hour, so for the most part the tables were practically empty. The baccarat table had not yet opened. The velvet rope was still strung across the opening in the railing, and the chairs were pushed up to the long table.

He angled left, walking down the two stairs and across to the bar, where he ordered cognac. He turned around and looked over the club, his back against the bar.

There were the usual few elderly ladies at the roulette wheels, and several American tourists stood at one of the blackjack tables. A couple of British naval officers were gambling at the craps table, and around the corner from the bar, a half-dozen men and three women, all dressed in evening clothes, were seated at a round table talking and laughing.

Carter almost missed him, his eyes sliding past, but then he casually looked that way again just as Juan Rojas raised a hand for the waitress. There was no mistaking the man.

Carter stared at him, willing him to turn to the left. And Rojas did, his eyes locking with Carter's. He nodded. Carter raised his snifter in salute, then turned back to the bar and lit a cigarette.

He took his time finishing his cognac, and when he was done, he turned the opposite way from where Rojas was seated with his friends and started toward one of the gaming tables.

Halfway across the floor, a short, very stocky man dressed in a well-tailored tuxedo approached him. "Mr. Carter?" he inquired politely.

Carter stopped and looked at the man for a long moment. "Who would like to know?" he said in a low voice, but it had a harsh, menacing edge to it.

The other man bridled. But he held himself in check.

"Senhor Juan Rojas—the man you saluted at the table back there—would like to buy you a drink, sir," the man explained in Portuguese-accented English.

"Rojas?" Carter asked, looking past the little man back toward the table. Everyone there, including Rojas, was looking his way. Rojas nodded again.

"Ah, *that* gentleman," Carter said. "But of course."

"You are Mr. Carter . . . ?" the stocky man started, but Carter brushed past him and headed over toward Rojas's table.

Rojas and the other men all stood as Carter approached. The three women looked up. They were all lovely, but the one seated at Rojas's left was particularly stunning.

Rojas held out his hand. "Mr. Carter, I believe?"

Carter nodded, and they shook hands.

"Welcome to London, sir. Permit me. I am Juan Rojas."

Carter grinned. "You have me at the disadvantage. I knew you, naturally. But tell me, how did you come to know who I am?"

Rojas laughed. "I have spies everywhere, Mr. Carter."

"And what have your spies told you?"

"That you were spying on me. That you are well-to-do. And that you have come to London to seek some . . . I believe your word was 'action.' "

Carter smiled weakly. "Your spies seem to be better than mine. But essentially what they have told you is true." He glanced at the ladies. "But please forgive me, sir. The only reason I spied at all was to find someone who might challenge what I might consider a certain skill with cards."

"What sort of cards, might I ask?" Rojas asked. He was intrigued.

"Poker," Carter said, naming the one game unexpected in these circles.

"How very . . . North American," Rojas said, a touch of

hardness creeping into his voice. "But tell me, Mr. Carter, how long do you plan on staying in London?" He motioned for Carter to have a seat at the table.

When they were all settled and all had fresh drinks, Carter turned back to Rojas. "My plans at this moment are indefinite, Senhor Rojas."

"Upon what do your plans depend, Mr. Carter?" the girl to Rojas's left asked.

"Permit me to introduce Senhorita Carmella Perez," Rojas said.

"Senhorita Perez," Carter said, inclining his head. He smiled. "My stay here is dependent upon only one thing."

"Which is?" the woman asked.

"Whether or not I find a gambler man enough to challenge me at my own game."

Rojas stiffened.

"I am looking for—if the ladies will please pardon my expression—a man with the balls to gamble with me."

Carmella hid her smile behind an ornate lace fan. Her eyes were very large and very dark.

Carter tossed down his remaining cognac, then stood up and bowed deeply to Rojas. "If you will now excuse me, Senhor Rojas, ladies and gentlemen. Thank you for the drink and the very pleasant company." The last he had directed to Carmella.

Rojas was angry. Carter could see it in the way the man abruptly got to his feet. It looked as if his bodyguards wanted nothing more than to yank out their artillery and blow Carter away.

"Where will you be . . . looking for your action this evening, Mr. Carter?" Rojas said. It sounded more like a command than a question.

Carter smiled and took his time answering. "I thought I might wander out to the Alhambra."

Rojas nodded. A faint sheen of **perspiration** covered his upper lip.

"I understand I might find **an amateur** or two out there," Carter added.

Rojas was visibly shaking.

"I'm told there's usually a high roller or two playing who fancies himself good but who couldn't win at a tea social even if his luck was with him.'

For just a moment Carter thought he had gone too far. The mountain of muscle next to Rojas started to reach inside his jacket. But Rojas held the man off with a glance, then turned to Carter with a tight smile that looked more like a grimace.

"Poker, you say?"

Carter stepped away from the table and held out his hand. Rojas took it reluctantly.

"Poker is my game," Carter admitted. "But I've been known to stoop so low as to meddle with a bit of chemin de fer."

"Baccarat?"

Carter laughed. "A ladies' game, actually. But I've played it from time to time."

THREE

At the front desk, Carter asked if there were any messages for him. In the glass front of the cabinet behind the long counter, Carter could see the reflection of two of Rojas's gorillas. They hung back by the bell captain's desk. They obviously had been sent to follow him.

"No, sir. No messages this evening."

"Thank you," Carter said. "I would like an automobile."

"Of course, sir. Your driver will be with you—"

"No," Carter said sharply. A few heads turned his way. "I would prefer a self-drive."

The clerk seemed flustered for just a moment. "I would not advise that, sir."

"I've been to London before, and I've driven here."

"As you wish, sir," the clerk said. He turned away and got on the phone. As he did, Carter watched the glass and saw Rojas, the three women with him, and his other four bodyguards emerge from the casino and leave the hotel by the front entrance. The two bodyguards who had evidently been assigned to Carter remained in the lobby.

The clerk put down the telephone and turned back to Carter. "A small Mercedes—I believe it will be a 450SL— will be at your disposal momentarily, sir."

Carter smiled. "Thank you. I'll be at the Alhambra." He placed a twenty-pound note on the counter, turned, and headed across the lobby. Out of the corner of his eye he noticed with satisfaction that one of his tails was scrambling toward a side door, while the other came his way.

Outside, a minute or two later, his tail hurried up the block and climbed into a Jaguar sedan with some kind of a shield on its radiator. A minute after that, a powder blue Mercedes 450SL convertible slid up to the curb, and a uniformed hotel employee jumped out.

"Mr. Carter?" he called.

Carter crossed the sidewalk and climbed into the car, passing the driver a ten-pound tip. The man closed the door.

"Now be careful driving, sir. The traffic is a bit fierce out there this evening."

"Right," Carter said through the open window. He slammed the car in low gear and hammered the accelerator pedal to the floor.

The Jaguar's lights came on, and the car leaped away from the curb, but within seconds Carter was careening around Piccadilly Circus much too fast, up Regent Street, and then West on Oxford Street toward Hyde Park.

Rojas's goons never had a chance. They had lost Carter from the moment he had pulled away from the hotel.

Down on Bayswater Road, Carter pulled into a side street where he doused the lights and parked. He wasn't too far from Paddington Station.

He locked the car and hurried up to the station on foot, where he quickly found a cab and directed the driver to take him to the Ritz.

Much to the cabby's puzzlement, Carter got out a block before the hotel and paid a very handsome tip. *Yanks're bloody crazy,* the driver thought, folding the money and putting it into a pocket.

After the cab had gone, Carter made his way around to a side entrance to the hotel. He climbed a flight of stairs to the third floor, where he took an elevator the rest of the way to the top floor.

Rojas and his men—except for the two still out looking for Carter—were on their way to the Alhambra. Carter figured Rojas's suite would be unattended this evening, at least for a few hours.

There were four penthouse suites on the top floor, and it took Carter only a few minutes to find out which belonged to Rojas. Two were occupied and had parties in progress. The third was empty; it was being redecorated. Which left the fourth. The front unit. The most prestigious of them all.

He used his stiletto to pick the easy lock, then he slipped inside. For a minute he just waited in the vestibule, listening to the sounds of the apartment.

Lamps had been left on in the sitting room, and there was light in what appeared to be a kitchenette and serving area on the inside wall. But there were no sounds. If anyone was still in the suite, he was either sleeping or very much on guard.

Carter withdrew his Luger, screwed the silencer on the barrel, and advanced carefully into the suite. The living room was clear, as was the front bathroom and second bedroom.

He slipped around the corner, down the short corridor, and into the master suite. The big bed had been slept in, and clothing had been tossed carelessly around it. But there was no one there. Nor was there anyone in the huge walk-in closets or in the master bath.

He unscrewed the silencer and reholstered his weapon, then went to work. Beginning with the master bath and efficiently working his way back toward the front door, he quietly searched the suite.

Carter found nothing of interest except for two names scrawled on the pad by the telephone in the master suite:

CHÂTEAU LE FAVRE
BARNET

Barnet was a small town just north of London. But Château Le Favre? Carter thought about the name, but it didn't ring a bell. Was it in England? Or perhaps France?

Carter took one last look around the suite to make sure he had not moved anything out of place, and then he went to the door. He opened it a crack and looked out into the corridor.

The bell captain was there with one of Rojas's men. It was one of the men who had followed Carter from the lobby. They were arguing about something and had evidently just come up on the elevator. Carter figured it was a safe bet they would come into the suite.

Carter closed and latched the door, hurried across the sitting room, and let himself out onto the balcony.

Far below, traffic on Piccadilly was heavy. Above, there was no way to the roof, which, even if he stood on the railing, was too far to reach.

Lights came on in the sitting room, and the sound of the voices of Rojas's man and the bell captain rose and fell.

Carter put his ear to the door.

". . . despite what you may have to say, Senhor Rojas told me to come back here and to stay here."

"I have no argument with that."

"You had better not," an angry voice shouted. "All you have to do is keep this floor clear."

"Impossible. This is a public hotel, not a private fortress."

"Then at least keep watch. If someone comes up, give me a call. If Carter—"

"If that bastard shows up here, I'll waste him," snapped the bell captain. "And you can tell that to your boss if you'd like. I don't care. He's nothing but a mouth with a lot of money. He's nothing to be worried about, I assure you."

Rojas's man laughed. "That is my worry, not yours. Just do as you are told, and when it is over you will be well paid."

"I want no trouble here."

"You will get none from me if you do as you are told."

There was silence for a while, but then Carter distinctly heard the front door to the suite open and close. A few minutes later the television came on.

Rojas's bodyguard was obviously going to remain in the suite for the rest of the night. There would be no getting past him without killing him, which would ruin everything. Getting to know Rojas and what he was up to wasn't going to be easy. Rojas would have to be convinced that Carter was nothing more than what he appeared to be: an arrogant playboy with far more money than sense.

Carter again checked the possibility of gaining access to the roof, but there was simply no way up. No decorative bricks to climb up. No downspouts. No wires. Nothing.

The sitting room balcony was separated from the master suite balcony by a space of about ten feet. Directly below that balcony was the balcony of the room on the floor below. It was a drop of around fifteen feet, and it was angled to the left.

Quickly, Carter stepped over the railing and, holding on with one hand, leaned way out and leaped for the master suite balcony, making it easily.

He stepped over that railing, went to the far side of the balcony, and looked over the edge.

There was a light shining from the window below, casting its pale yellow glow on the narrow strip of concrete.

There was no other way. Carter took a few deep breaths. The street was six stories below. A very long drop.

He climbed over the railing, then, hunching down, eased his body over the edge. He started swinging, first in short little arcs, then going wider and wider, his movements pulling his hands from the balcony floor.

At the precise moment he was certain his grip would no longer hold, he gave one final swing and dropped off into space.

The balcony came up beneath him, and he hit feet first but off-balance, striking the railing painfully with his left forearm and chest.

He straightened up just as the curtains were yanked back in Rojas's suite above. The balcony door opened, and someone stepped out.

Carter flattened himself against the far corner of his balcony. From where he stood he could just see the edge of Rojas's balcony. A pair of shoes and trouser legs appeared, stopped a moment, then went away. The balcony door closed, and it was quiet again.

Carter breathed a sigh of relief, then put his ear against the door. He thought he could hear running water—maybe a shower—and he could hear someone talking. After a minute or so he realized the talking was the television, and the running water was indeed a shower.

He tried the balcony door. It was unlocked and slid back easily. He parted the curtain and looked inside.

A black slip and a black cocktail dress were laid out on the king-size bed. The bathroom door was open.

Carter slipped into the room, closing the balcony door behind him, and made his way across the room to the bathroom door.

The shower stopped as he stepped past the open door. He could hear the door of the shower stall opening, and a woman started to hum some tune.

He opened the door to the hotel corridor and looked out for a second. He was just turning back after closing the door when an attractive young woman stepped out of the bathroom.

She stopped in her tracks. Startled. And nude.

Carter smiled. "Pardon me, miss, but apparently I have the wrong room. Either that or I have a beautiful albeit unknown visitor."

She smiled back. "You have the wrong room, unfortunately, Monsieur . . . ?" She was French.

"I'm so sorry," Carter said. He turned, hurried down the corridor, and pushed the button for the elevator. Before the car came he looked back. The woman was peering around the corner of the doorframe.

"*Au revoir,*" he said as he stepped into the elevator and the doors closed.

His chest hurt, and his arm ached. He didn't think he had broken anything. But he'd be sore as hell in the morning.

He got off on the ballroom floor, then crossed to the back where he took a service elevator to the ground floor and let himself out the back way.

A few of the hotel staff saw him, but no one paid him any attention. A block away he hailed a cab, which he took back to Paddington Station. From there he walked back to the Mercedes.

Forty minutes later Carter pulled up in front of the Alhambra. It was ten o'clock, and he was very hungry and very sore.

"Welcome to the Alhambra," an olive-skinned valet greeted him as he got out of the car. Cuban? Carter wondered as he started through the gates and up the walk.

He was ready to meet Rojas tonight. The man was here to gamble. Carter would give it to him. His plan was to gently hammer at the man and to keep hammering at him until something popped, until Rojas made a mistake.

He was greeted at the door by the club manager. "Welcome to the Alhambra, sir. Are you a member?"

"Yes," Carter said. "But this will be my first visit."

"I see, sir," the manager said. He was about to show Carter to the registration desk, when he stopped. "Your name, sir?"

"Carter. Nick Carter. You may contact the Ritz for my—"

"That will not be necessary, sir. Senhor Rojas has vouched for you. He is expecting you."

Carter just looked at the man.

"Sir?" the manager asked.

"I'd just as soon you check with the Ritz in town. I'm nobody's guest here but my own. Especially not Senhor Rojas's."

"Of course, sir," the man said smoothly. He had been down this path with other guests. He picked up a telephone, asked for a number, and within two minutes he was hanging up, a huge smile on his face. "What sort of a line will you be needing this evening, Mr. Carter?"

"A hundred thousand for now. And a dealer."

"Pounds, sir?"

"Of course. And we'll be playing poker." Carter wrote a check for that amount.

"Yes, sir."

"I drink cognac. Good cognac."

"Of course. And will you and Senhor Rojas be needing a private room?"

Carter appeared to think about it for a moment, but then he shook his head. "No, I don't believe so. Let's make this public. It should be educational."

Carter went through the entrance hall, up three stairs, and into the main gaming room. It was very large, and unlike Las Vegas rooms with their low ceilings, this one had high, soaring ceilings with huge chandeliers, making it seem almost like a church.

Slot machines were to the left, blackjack and craps tables

were straight ahead, and to the right were the roulette wheels. Beyond them stood the baccarat tables, two of them.

A band was set up along the back wall, and on the near wall to the right was the bar. To the left were three special gaming tables. One of them was being set up now.

Rojas was nowhere to be seen. Carter got himself a cognac from the bar and wandered off to the right, toward the roulette tables.

The woman who had been with Rojas was there. She was winning. Carter stood behind her for a minute or two before she turned and looked up at him.

"Mr. Carter," she said. Her voice was as lovely as she was.

"Senhorita Perez, I believe it is."

She smiled and inclined her head. "You are here to see Juan?"

"Yes, I am."

"He is most anxious to meet with you at the gaming tables," she said. Without looking, she placed large bets on black and on even.

"And this makes you nervous?"

"Somewhat," she said, smiling softly. "Juan is . . . how shall I say . . . a very intense man. For him now, winning is everything. He would stop at nothing, Mr. Carter, at nothing."

"Does he cheat?"

"I never cheat, sir, but I always win."

Carter turned around to face the tall, handsome South American. They shook hands.

"I understand you wish to play a little poker."

"The thought had crossed my mind on the way out here."

"Did you have trouble finding the place?"

"None whatsoever, Senhor Rojas. I drove right to it."

It was all Rojas could do to maintain his self-control. His

goons behind him looked as if they wanted to take the place apart.

"A thousand-pound ante and a three-raise limit suit you?" Carter asked.

"Twenty-five hundred pounds might be better," Rojas replied, smiling.

Carter looked back at Carmella, whose eyes were wide. He turned back to Rojas.

"Is it high-stakes poker you're after, then?"

"Exactly," Rojas replied.

Carter let the smile fade from his lips. "Then let's cut the bullshit, Rojas," he said, his voice soft, and low, and menacing. "Ten-thousand-pound ante with no raise limit. Just you and me and the dealer. No one else."

Rojas was taken aback. There were several people gathered around them now that it was understood some kind of a gambling duel was in the offing. Rojas finally nodded.

"Good," Carter said, brushing past the man and his gorillas and heading toward the poker table. "I'm just in the mood to kick some ass tonight."

A young man dressed in a tuxedo was seated behind the dealer's position at the table that had been set up for them. The club manager was standing nearby to make sure everything would go smoothly.

Carter stalked up to the table and stopped by his chair.

The young dealer was dark-haired and very good-looking. Carter would have bet his last dollar the man was Cuban. Rojas was dealing with the Russians on this one, and something was about to happen in the Caribbean basin. Cuba and Russia were close allies.

Carter decided to take this opportunity to again shake up Rojas and his people.

"You," he said to the dealer. "Get out of there. Get away from the table."

The young man was shocked. He stood up but didn't move away.

"I said I want you to get the hell out of there. Don't you understand English?"

The club manager rushed up to Carter. Rojas and his people stood aside, watching.

"Sir, what is the trouble?"

"I don't want this man as my dealer," Carter snapped.

The manager started to sputter something, but Carter cut him off.

"I just don't like his looks."

"Of course, sir," the manager said, recovering his composure. "Do you have anyone in mind? We can bring in another dealer."

"I want you," Carter said. The man was British, and the club would rise or fall on his honesty. Whereas one of his dealers might be able to get away with something and not seriously hurt the club's reputation, its manager could not.

"Impossible, sir," the man said.

But Carter had already seated himself. "I would like another cognac," he said, holding up his glass. "And I would like to begin. I am here to play cards, not argue."

"But Mr. Carter, it is impossible for me to act as your dealer. I have many other duties."

Carter looked from the man to Rojas. "What say, Senhor Rojas?" he called out, deliberately mispronouncing the man's name.

Rojas went white. His bodyguards were shaking with ambition, but Rojas held them back. He nodded to the manager.

"It would be a personal favor to me, Mr. Danners."

The manager looked from Rojas to Carter and back again. Finally he nodded. "As you wish, gentlemen. The Alhambra is here to serve."

"I wonder where I've heard that line before?" Carter mumbled under his breath but loud enough for the crowd nearest him to hear what he said.

Rojas sat down, his bodyguards on either side of him, two of his girls nearby.

Danners, the club manager, took his seat, passed a sealed deck to each man for their inspection, and then opened one.

Deftly he spread the cards out in the perfect dealer's arc, then flipped them over in a fan, smoothly extracting the jokers.

"Mr. Carter, you named the action, which makes you the challenger," Danners said. He turned to Rojas. "Senhor Rojas, it is up to you to name the game."

"Five card stud," Rojas said without hesitation. "First and last card up, bets double on the first pair or better."

Carter grinned. He glanced at his chips. "Golds are ten thousand pounds, reds are five thousand, and blue, a thousand?"

Danners nodded, passing the shuffled deck to Carter, who cut. Danners smoothly closed the deck and quickly dealt the first cards as Carmella Perez came up behind Carter and lit a cigarette.

FOUR

It was just a little after midnight. A fairly large crowd had gathered behind Rojas and Carter at the poker table where Claude Danners, the Alhambra's manager, was dealing.

Rojas had been winning quite heavily. At this point he was at least £150,000 ahead. Carter had had to write a check for a second £100,000.

There was already a certain pessimism in the crowd, that was common in any totally one-sided contest. Rojas had begun by winning, he had continued to win, and it looked as if nothing would stop him.

But Carter had let the man win. As far as he was able to tell, Danners had not cheated. But Carter suspected that had the handsome Hispanic dealt, there would have been no question who was going to win.

Rojas had begun as a conservative gambler in an unfamiliar game against an unfamiliar player.

Early on, however, after Carter had had a couple of very desultory wins and some fairly heavy losses, Rojas had begun to smile and enjoy himself. He had loosened up immediately, swinging his bets wide, searching for fills for his pairs and triplets for his full houses.

It was time, Carter figured, to teach the man a little bit about poker.

Danners had just dealt the first cards up: a king for Rojas and an ace for Carter. The second card, down, came, and Carter, without bothering to look at it, slid a pile of chips across.

"Ace bets fifty thousand," he said.

Rojas blinked and stiffened. A slight stir rustled through the crowd.

"The man has a pair of aces," Rojas said, matching the bet. The previous largest bet had only been £20,000. With the antes, there was £120,000 in the center of the table now, with only two of the five cards out.

"The table is set?" Danners asked.

Carter nodded. Rojas grinned and nodded.

The third card each, down, came out. Still Carter did not bother looking at his two down cards.

"Ace bets another fifty thousand," Carter said.

The crowd murmured.

Danners sat forward. "I am sorry, Mr. Carter, but you have exceeded your credit limit."

"You are going to stop me with a hand like this?"

"But you have not even looked at your cards, sir!"

"You are going to tell me how to play poker, then?" Carter snapped. He reached for his wallet. Rojas's goons nearly jumped out of their tuxedoes. But Carter pulled out his wallet, opened it, and tossed out his three premier credit cards. "Between them, I have a credit limit of a million and a half . . . *pounds*. More if I wish to make a call. Do you wish to challenge my marker?"

Danners scooped up Carter's credit cards. "I am most sorry, sir. I meant no disrespect. Of course your marker is good with the Alhambra."

Carter smiled. "Thank you. The ace bets fifty thousand, as I was saying."

Danners passed over £250,000 in gold markers, and Carter diverted £50,000 to the center of the table.

Rojas checked his down cards, smiled ever so slightly, and shoved out five £10,000 markers. "See your fifty thousand," he said and pushed out two more. "And raise you twenty thousand more."

The entire club was deathly silent, except for an occasional slot machine. Someone in the back was oblivious to the drama at the table.

Carter laughed out loud. "The man has spirit. I like that!" He shoved out £20,000. "See your twenty"—he shoved out five more gold markers—"and raise you another fifty thousand."

A gasp ran through the crowd. Rojas looked at his down cards again. Carter lit a cigarette and ordered another cognac. His eyes met Carmella's. She looked very frightened.

The moment stretched for a long time. Carter's drink came even though it was illegal to drink at a gaming table.

"A bet has been placed, Senhor Rojas," Danners finally said. His voice was soft and very obsequious.

"I see it," Rojas snarled. He shoved five gold markers into the huge pile at the center of the table.

"No raises, Senhor Rojas?" Carter taunted.

"Let's play poker."

Carter nodded.

Danners dealt the fourth card, the last one down, and sat back. Rojas eased his card up so that he could just see it. He brightened ever so slightly. Carter figured the man had a pair of kings. Anything better and he'd be betting more heavily than he had been, just on the come.

Carter made a show of not looking at his down cards, and he shoved out another £50,000. "Ace bets fifty big ones."

Rojas grinned. "I'll see that and raise you another fifty,"

he said, shoving ten gold chips across.

"I was right. A pair of kings and the man gets frisky."
Carter shoved a huge pile of chips across. "See your fifty
thousand—and raise you a hundred grand."

One could almost touch the tension in the atmosphere of
the club. Even Danners, whom Carter was sure had seen a lot
of gambling in his time, was on his toes. In the center of the
table rested £ 660,000. And there was more to come.

Rojas leaned back and spoke with one of his goons for a
moment. The man and one of his buddies peeled off from the
crowd and left. Trouble, Carter figured.

Very slowly Rojas pushed across the £ 100,000 raise. "I'll
hold here," he said.

"The table set, gentlemen?" Danners asked.

Rojas nodded.

"You're not so proud of your pair of kings, *senhor*?"
Carter asked with an American twang, mangling his pronun-
ciation of the Portuguese word.

"Let's play cards," Rojas snapped.

"I thought that's what I was doing," Carter said innocently, sitting forward. He motioned for the next card.

Danners dealt Carter a second ace, and Rojas a queen. The
South American seemed confused for a moment, then
crestfallen, and finally he sat back and just looked at Carter, a
very odd look in his eyes.

Carter chuckled. "Pair of aces bets a hundred thousand,
and he hopes for a substantial raise from the peanut gallery."

Rojas looked at his down cards. A thin sheen of perspiration coated his brow. He looked up at Carter. "You play this
without looking at your cards?"

Carter slammed his hand on the tabletop. "Is everyone in
this goddamned club going to tell me how to play poker?"

Rojas said nothing. Danners looked away. The crowd was
excited.

"Play," Carter whispered. "Bet or fold, I don't give a damn."

"I think you have the third ace," Rojas said calmly.

"You'll have to pay to see it, *senhor*. One hundred grand." There was £860,000 on the table.

Rojas had less than £20,000 in chips left. He was good for more. Everyone believed that. He toyed with the chips for a bit.

"You going to play poker or count your money?" Carter asked.

Rojas smiled and shook his head. "Too much for me," he said. He flipped his cards down and shoved them toward Danners. "I need another few hundred thousand. The next hand will be better."

Carter grinned and stood up. The crowd gasped. He tossed a £10,000 chip toward Danners, another illegal move under British law. "Thanks for an interesting game. Send my winnings over to the Ritz."

Rojas jumped up. "You're not quitting now . . ."

"Indeed I am," Carter said pleasantly. "I always make it a practice to quit while I'm ahead. You should take a lesson, Senhor Rojas."

One of Rojas's bodyguards had come around the table. He brushed past Carter and reached down for his hand, intending to turn over the three down cards. Carter's hand shot out, pinning the other man's hand to the table.

For a moment there was a little struggle that was mostly hidden from the spectators' view. Carter had the advantage in strength and, because of his position, in leverage.

Rojas nodded, and the bodyguard relaxed. For a long moment Carter held tight, a very hard look coming into his eyes.

"You ever attempt anything like that again with me, big boy, and I'll kill you."

Carter released the man's hand and stepped back, his muscles taut and ready for whatever the goon might take it into his head to do.

But the bodyguard had more control than Carter had given him credit for. He backed off, rubbing his wrist.

"I am sorry, sir. I apologize. I meant nothing. I was curious . . ."

Carter rudely turned away from him. "As I was saying, Mr. Danners, have my winnings sent to the Ritz."

Danners nodded. He was hoping for no trouble.

"And it would be unfortunate . . . most unfortunate if anything should happen to my funds between here and there."

Danners puffed up. "I assure you, sir—"

"Yes, you do," Carter said. He turned and bowed slightly to Carmella, then nonchalantly headed out of the club, the crowd parting with respect for him. No matter the establishment, to bet and win more than three quarters of a million pounds was an achievement.

Outside, a Mercedes sedan took off into the night, back toward London, and Carter grinned. The frontline troops, no doubt.

The parking valet came, saw Carter, and hurried back for his car. A minute or two later the 450SL slid up to the canopy, and the valet jumped out.

Carter got in behind the wheel, the door was closed, and he headed out, swinging around toward London. He figured he'd give them a couple of miles to do whatever it was they wanted to do before he'd double back.

He had hurt Rojas. He had seen it in the man's manner. Now he wanted to see what the Brazilian's reaction would be . . . other than sending his gorillas after the opposition, of course.

It happened less than two blocks from the club. The big

Mercedes was slewed across the road, its front right wheel just over the edge.

There was no one in sight. The road was very dark. Carter unbuttoned his jacket and came to a complete halt.

For a moment or two he just sat there, then he doused his headlights, leaving only his parking lights on, and he pulled his car over to the side of the road. He left himself plenty of room to get the hell out of there in a hurry if necessary.

He got out of the car and stepped around toward the Mercedes sedan some twenty feet away. The big car's headlights were on. As Carter got closer, he could see a man dressed in a tuxedo hunched over the steering wheel as if he had hit his head in the crash and was unconscious.

Carter didn't think they'd kill him. Not until they knew what he was all about. And not until they had a chance to get Rojas's money back. But they were going to rough him up.

Or at least they were going to try.

He came around the rear of the sedan and cautiously moved up to the open window on the driver's side. The man hunched over the steering wheel didn't move. Carter reached out and touched his shoulder, and the man sat up, a big Russian automatic in his right fist.

Carter stepped back, his hands going up, as someone else came out of the shadows in the trees beside the road.

The man in the car started to get out at the same moment the goon behind reached around for Carter's gun.

Carter stepped aside, knocking the man's gun away with his elbow, then turned, grabbed the second man, spun him around, and shoved him against the half-open car door.

"Son of a bitch," one of them shouted.

Carter stepped forward, his weight swinging to his left foot as he planted a right hook on the goon's chin.

The bodyguard's head snapped back, bouncing against the roof of the car, and he started to sink to his knees.

Carter grabbed his lapels and propelled him away from the car, sending him skidding on the roadway.

He yanked the car door the rest of the way open, reached inside, and pulled out the half-dazed "accident victim." He hit him once very hard in the solar plexus and again just as hard in the face. The man slumped to his knees and then fell on his face on the road.

Working quickly now, in case another car came along, Carter bent down and retrieved both men's guns and wallets.

Back in his own car, he swung the Mercedes sedan around and drove another half a block until he found a driveway in which to turn around. Then he headed back to the Alhambra.

Carter remained where he was, parked half a block from the front entrance to the club, for nearly an hour, smoking one cigarette after another. For a while he thought he had already missed Rojas. He figured the man had already left the club.

He had almost decided to risk going inside and looking around when Rojas, four of his bodyguards, and the three women, including Carmella Perez, came out of the club.

They stood there, laughing and talking, waiting for the valet to bring their car.

Carter was somewhat disappointed. He would have bet almost anything that a wounded Rojas, losing at cards, would head out without his entourage—or at least without most of it—to confer with whoever he was doing this for.

Actually, Carter thought, his logic was a little thin. Despite what AXE's files indicated, and despite their best predictions as to what Rojas was up to, the man could very well be here in London for nothing more than was apparent— merely to have a good time gambling.

Two cars pulled up to the curb, and two valets popped out. Carter grinned.

The women and all but one of the bodyguards got into the first limousine, and they left.

Rojas got into the passenger seat, and the remaining bodyguard slid behind the wheel of the second limo. They pulled out of the Alhambra's gate as the first limo flashed past Carter, then turned the opposite way and headed off into the night.

Carter waited until the limousine's taillights all but disappeared in the distance, and then he pulled away from the side of the road and headed after them.

For a time there was some doubt in his mind as to where Rojas and his man were going. But after they had gone way out to Newham—which was far to the east of London—they turned back to the northwest, and then he knew. They were headed up to Barnet. The Château Le Favre. When they hit the E8 and headed directly west, he was certain.

Carter took the next exit, unlimbering the 450SL through the silent, dark British countryside.

It was very late at night—or early in the morning, depending on your point of view—when Carter turned onto Wood Street, the main street of Barnet. There was absolutely no traffic stirring as he found a phone booth and looked through the directory for the Château Le Favre.

There was no listing.

He called information, but they had no listing for such a place either, the operator no doubt thinking Carter crazy for looking for a French restaurant at that hour.

He went back to his car and got behind the wheel. For a minute or two he remained there, staring vacantly at the phone booth.

It would actually be quite simple. He could call AXE in Washington and have them vouch for him here with the Barnet police. They would tell him what he wanted to know.

But that was too risky, given his orders. Rojas was not to know or even suspect that he wasn't what he presented himself to be. Nothing more than a very rich playboy. With incredible guts and even better luck.

Carter started the car and drove off, his mind working. It would have been too risky to have directly followed Rojas and his driver out here. Sooner or later they would have spotted the headlights behind them.

He drifted out toward the E8 where it came into town and merged with the other highways, and suddenly he had it.

He pulled into an all-night service station-restaurant, parked in the rear, and went into the restaurant.

As he had hoped, there was a gift shop for tourists to the area. Included was a magazine rack and book display. He found the book he was looking for almost immediately: *Homes of Note in Watford, Barnet and Cheshunt*. The Château Le Favre was listed in the index, as Carter suspected it might be.

The guide cost him more than three pounds. He took it back to the restaurant, where he ordered a cup of tea and a muffin with marmalade, and started reading.

The home had been built in the late 1600s in Lisieux in the Calvados region of France. In 1787 a terrible fire all but destroyed the twenty-seven-room mansion, but eleven years later it had been rebuilt by an attorney from Paris who had somehow managed to survive the terrible purges both during and after the Revolution.

In the late twenties the home was sold to a wealthy Indian, who had it carefully dismantled, brought to England, and reconstructed stone by stone on its present site near Barnet.

Since then, the Mansion had changed hands several times. It had been slightly damaged during the Second World War, had been opened as a mental hospital in the early fifties, and since 1977 had been maintained as a private residence by an

Arab gentleman originally from Kuwait. His telephone was unlisted.

The house was situated on 150 acres of hilly, heavily wooded land that had once been a game preserve of King Richard the Lion-Hearted.

Carter finished his snack, paid, and left. The mansion was way out on Axeton Manor Road to the west of town, and the book gave explicit directions for how to find it. Fifteen minutes later he was passing a small signboard, attached to a rockpile, that announced LE FAVRE.

He drove on for another few hundred yards before he pulled over to the side of the road and parked the car in a wide, grassy ditch. He pocketed the keys and headed up through the woods, angling back toward the driveway he had passed.

He crossed a low, barbed wire fence—highly unusual for England, Carter noted—and the land climbed gently from the low, flat area through which the highway had run. At the crest of a hill, Carter looked down on the Château Le Favre. The house was very large, with dormers, chimneys, and balconies to either side of the main entrance and along the sides.

Several cars were parked out front, including the limousine in which Rojas and his bodyguard had left the Alhambra.

For a minute or two Carter remained where he was, studying the house and its grounds. But there was little to be seen. There was no movement. No one came or went. And only the windows in the front right rooms were lit. All else was in darkness.

Finally Carter made his way down the hill, crossing the road well back from the house so that if anyone were on guard duty, he would not be seen.

It took him fifteen minutes to work his way around to the

side of the house and then up beneath the front right balcony, where he managed to get to one of the windows.

Through the gap in the drapes, Carter could see Rojas seated with two other men. Both of them looked hard, weatherbeaten, but both of them were dressed to the nines.

They had familiar faces, but Carter did not recognize them. They looked almost like soldiers to him, with their erect bearing, their short haircuts, and their direct motions.

Rojas had a briefcase that he stood up and opened on the big oak desk.

One of the other men pulled something out of the briefcase, and Carter got a good look at it.

It was money. A bundle of money. British pounds. If the briefcase was filled with money, there was a lot there.

Rojas was delivering money to these men. But who were they? And for what was the money payment?

Carter stared at the two men for a long time, memorizing their faces, before he left the window.

FIVE

Carter went around to the back of the house, then crossed a narrow courtyard behind the garage, where he slipped into the shadows and crouched down.

From where he was he could see the back of the house, and beyond the west side he could see the driveway that led out to the highway.

When Rojas left, Carter would know it.

The weather was cool that morning, and a few clouds began to float across the star-studded sky. Finally it began to drizzle, a desultory, chilly rain that soon soaked Carter to the skin.

It was after four in the morning when Rojas's limousine finally left, and a half hour after that before the lights in the house all went out.

Carter waited until five, then he moved from his hiding place, crossed the courtyard, and came up to one of the rear entrances to the house.

Through a window beside the door he could see a short corridor that led into what appeared to be a pantry. Canned goods and other foodstuffs were stacked on shelves. A doorway beyond seemed to lead into the kitchen.

The door was locked with a deadbolt, but as far as Carter could tell, the window was not alarmed.

He wrapped the butt of his Luger in his handkerchief and carefully broke one of the windowpanes near the sash lock, then removed the fragments of glass.

Quickly he unlatched the window, slid it up, and climbed inside. He turned, went through the pantry, and stepped into the kitchen.

It was a very large room, with the professional equipment needed for cooking banquet-sized meals. Directly across from where he stood were the large serving doors that apparently led into the dining room. To the right was another, narrower door that probably led to the rest of the house.

He silently crossed the kitchen, put his ear to the narrower door, and listened. If anyone had heard the breaking glass, which he felt was highly unlikely, they'd have been stirring by now. But there were no sounds from the house other than what he took to be the ticking of a large clock.

The door opened onto a long vestibule from which narrow stairs rose to the second floor—the servants' staircase, Carter guessed—and which led to the main hallway at the front of the house.

Carter turned from the stairs and followed the corridor to the front, where he stopped again to listen in the shadows at the foot of the main staircase.

A grandfather clock chimed the half hour in the living room to the right.

The study, where he had seen Rojas hand over the money to the other men, was to the left. Entry was through a set of double doors with wide brass hinges, long handles, and a very large, ornately tooled lock.

It took Carter less than half a minute to spring the two-hundred-year-old lock with his stiletto, and he pushed open the doors, stepped into the study, and silently closed and relocked them.

There was almost no light in the study. Carter took out his penlight, aimed it in the general direction of the desk, and flashed it on.

He got the brief impression of a large man seated behind the desk. The man's arm was coming up when Carter's penlight went out. Carter rolled left, diving for the floor.

The characteristically soft *plop* of a silenced weapon sounded twice, once to the right where Carter had been and then just inches away from Carter's right leg as he rolled once again, then lay perfectly still.

Carter slipped his stiletto out of his sleeve, then held his breath as a rustle of fabric came from behind the desk. A floorboard creaked, then was quiet.

For what seemed like a very long time, Carter remained lying where he was, not moving a muscle. The other man was doing the same. He was a professional. In the brief moment Carter had seen the man's face, he had recognized him as one of the two men to whom Rojas had handed the money. Short-cropped hair. Weatherbeaten complexion. The look of a hard man. And now this.

It would not be long before the dawn came, and then this game of hide and seek in the darkness would be over for both of them. It would become increasingly difficult for Carter to get out of the house and return to his car without being detected.

The entire operation could go down the tubes at this point if Rojas knew for a fact that Carter was something other than what he presented himself to be. If someone saw him leaving this place and could identify him, Rojas would bolt.

Which meant one thing. The man across the desk was going to have to die. And within the next minute or so.

Carter turned his head toward the door, cupped his mouth with his free hand, and coughed once. In the darkness even a pro would be fooled by the direction of the sound.

The gunman fired two shots toward the door, the muzzle flash just barely visible through the silencer barrel.

Carter rose to his knees and threw the stiletto in that direction. The gunman grunted, then fired two more shots in Carter's direction, but Carter had swung farther left and ducked below the level of the desk.

Again the study was absolutely silent.

Carter had hit the man with the razor-sharp blade. He knew that for a fact. But it could have been a superficial wound, perhaps in the man's arm or leg.

He reached carefully inside his tuxedo for his holstered Luger, then inside his pocket for the silencer. He was screwing the silencer onto the end of the barrel when something hit the desk. He nearly jumped out of his skin.

Some papers and what sounded like a book were shoved from the desk, and then the gunman presumably sank to the floor with a soft groan.

Carter finished screwing the silencer onto Wilhelmina as he slowly stood up. Holding the automatic in his right hand, his penlight in his left, he silently eased himself around the desk.

When he was in position, he flipped the light on for just an instant, then feinted right. But it wasn't necessary. The gunman lay on his side, his eyes open, his hands clawing at the stiletto buried to the haft just below his sternum. There was a lot of blood down the front of his white shirt.

Once around the back of the desk, Carter laid down his Luger and knelt beside the body. He studied the man's features. Somehow the man looked familiar. Or perhaps his face was just a type that Carter had seen before.

He eased Hugo out of the man's chest and carefully wiped

the blade on the man's shirt, then sheathed it, first making absolutely sure there was no blood left on the knife or on his hands. Should any blood be on his own shirt or jacket, Carter knew he would not be able to get back into the hotel without word getting back to Rojas.

He rolled the man over and searched his pockets. But there was nothing other than a cigarette lighter inscribed *To BPK with love LB*, and a pack of Players cigarettes.

A quick search of the desk revealed nothing of interest either. Whoever worked at the desk appeared to be an ordinary banker or investment counselor. The drawers were filled with corporate portfolios and reports. The appointment book contained cryptic messages for meetings, a few of which Carter was able to decipher as meetings at or about various London and Paris banking establishments.

The only single item of interest was found in one of the side drawers. It was an English-Arabic dictionary. A well-thumbed dictionary. Whoever worked at this desk, and Carter strongly suspected it was not the man he had just done battle with, evidently dealt with the Arabs on a regular basis. Investing their money, it appeared.

So what was the gunman doing here? Rojas, Carter could understand. A man of his business interests and stature would no doubt have plenty of cause to know whoever owned this place. But not the man lying here dead.

Carter picked up his Luger and went over to the windows, where he eased the curtains back and looked outside. Already to the east there was a perceptible lightening of the sky. It would be dawn soon. And with the dawn would come the end of his chances for getting out of here undetected.

There would be something here in the house that would tell him something. He was almost certain of it. But he had run out of time.

The windows swung outward. Carter opened them and

stepped out onto the veranda. He reached back inside and made sure the curtains were closed as before, then shut the windows. He was unable to relock them. But he figured it would most likely go unnoticed.

He made his way directly across the driveway, then into the woods and up the hill.

It was raining again, this time very hard by the time he climbed over the barbed wire fence and made it down to where he had parked the Mercedes in the grassy ditch.

He got into the car, started the engine, and eased back up onto the highway heading back toward Barnet.

It was pushing eight o'clock, and the morning traffic was horrendous by the time Carter made it back to the Ritz and turned his car in at the front door.

He had loosened his tie, and he staggered up the steps and into the lobby, the doorman's eyebrows raising.

Carter figured there'd be no way he could have made it into the hotel at this hour without running into one of the staff, no matter which entrance he used. And if he had been caught sneaking around, questions were bound to be asked, questions that would most certainly get back to Rojas.

He was walking a tightrope here. If he stumbled and fell, it would mean the end of this operation and possibly even his own death.

It was better, he had figured, to enter the hotel openly.

He stumbled halfway across the lobby and nearly fell. A bellman rushed across and took him by the elbow.

"Here, sir, let me give you a hand," the man said.

"What the hell's the matter with you?" Carter snapped, pulling his arm away. He straightened up—as if he had just noticed where he was—and resolutely, but still unsteadily, made his way the rest of the way across the lobby. He got his key at the desk.

"Any messages?" he asked.

The clerk's nostrils flared. "No, Mr. Carter, there are no messages, although there has been a rather . . . substantial deposit to your account with our cashier here."

"That's good," Carter said loudly. "If there're two things I can't stand, it's cheats and poor sports."

"Yes, sir. Shall I have some coffee sent up to your suite?"

Carter laughed. "Why not? And send me up some bacon and eggs, and spuds too. A little o.j. and maybe some toast. Thanks."

He turned and made his way to the elevator, where he leaned against the back wall as the doors slid shut and the car started up.

"Bit 'o luck, sir?" the elderly elevator operator asked pleasantly.

Carter grinned. "You're damned tootin' I had some luck. Took Rojas to the cleaners."

"So I heard, sir."

"Did you hear why I won so big?" Carter slurred his words.

They had come to his floor, and the doors were sliding open. "No, sir, I hadn't," the elevator man said, turning to him.

Carter pushed away from the wall and sauntered off the car. " 'Cause that wily South American couldn't cheat, that's why."

Carter could almost hear the old man gasp as the elevator doors slid shut and the car went back down.

There was no one in the corridor as Carter hurried to his room and let himself in. He peeled off his sodden tuxedo and left it in a heap. His weapons, along with the weapons and wallets he had taken from the men who had tried to waylay him on the road near the Alhambra, went into a drawer.

He took a quick shower, then shaved. He was just finishing

dressing when room service arrived with his breakfast.

Still feigning drunkenness, Carter tipped the man excessively, and had him take away his tuxedo and formal pumps for cleaning.

When he was alone again, he wolfed down his breakfast, then poured himself a stiff shot of cognac and lit a cigarette. He was very tired, but he was entirely too keyed up to sleep just yet.

Meanwhile, the opening salvos had been fired. He had prodded Rojas, and the Brazilian had struck back. It was going to be interesting to see what the repercussions would be after the morning's incident out at the Château Le Favre.

But Carter wasn't going to wait for that. He was going to push Rojas again.

He strapped on his own weapons, pocketed the guns and wallets from Rojas's two goons, and left his room.

Holding himself stiffly erect, he made his way across the lobby as a drunken man might who had just taken a shower and was trying to be on his very best behavior.

He turned a few heads, he knew, and he suspected that a pair of Rojas's men fell in behind him.

Outside, Carter had the doorman hail him a taxi, and he had the driver take him to the Albert Memorial at the edge of Kensington Gardens just west of Hyde Park.

He got out, entered the park, and within a hundred yards he doubled back in time to see Rojas's men racing up the path he had just taken.

Back out on Kensington Road, he hailed a passing taxi and was gone before his two tails knew what had happened. He figured they'd be in the park for most of the rest of the morning.

Carter took the cab to the north side of Regents Park, then he walked to the St. John's Wood underground station, doubling back three times to make sure he wasn't being followed before he scurried below and jumped on a train heading back toward Piccadilly.

He switched trains at Oxford Circus and got off at the Bond Street station, then hurried through the streets to Grosvenor Square to the U.S. embassy.

There were a number of people in the waiting room, including one vociferous woman who was threatening dire action against the ambassador and even the President if need be.

Carter picked up a phone on one of the vacant desks and dialed the ambassador's office.

"Four-two-one," his secretary answered.

One of the embassy staff had spotted Carter using the phone, and he broke away from a discussion with three young women and started across the room.

"This is Nick Carter. Please tell Mr. Leland that I am here in the embassy. I must speak with him immediately."

"Who is this?" the secretary demanded.

"Just be a dear and pass my message along to Ziggy," Carter said, using the nickname known only to a handful of people.

The secretary gasped. But then she said, "Please hold one moment, Mr. Carter."

"Surely," Carter said, and he looked up as the embassy employee, a young man wearing a corduroy suit, approached.

"Excuse me, but what do you think you're doing? These aren't public telephones—"

"May I help you, sir?" Carter asked pleasantly.

The young man sputtered. "Help *me*? What do you think you're doing—"

"I'm working. Now, may I help you, Mr. . . . .?"

"Hodgkiss," he said, then sputtered something else, but Carter held him off as the ambassador's secretary, now a completely diffident woman, came on the line.

"Mr. Carter, sir?"

"I'm still here."

"Mr. Leland will see you immediately."

"Will you send someone down for me?"

"Have one of the staffers bring you up, sir."

"Right," Carter said, and he hung up the phone. "Hodgkiss, my lad, we're off to see the ambassador."

"What?"

Carter took the young man by the elbow and steered him across the reception area to the elevators. "Which way?"

"Up, fourth floor, but you can't go up there without an appointment."

"I have one," Carter said, punching the button for the elevator.

Ambassador George Leland took Carter into his office and dismissed a very surprised Hodgkiss. Inside, with the door closed, Leland poured them both some coffee.

"Still can't get used to tea at this hour of the morning . . ." the ambassador began.

"Is this room secure, sir?"

Leland looked at him sharply, but a second later he nodded. "Yes, it is. It's swept every morning."

"What have you been told about my job here, sir?"

"Not much, Carter, other than that you'd be here and to give you a hand if necessary. I'm assuming you're in need of some assistance now?"

"Just a large padded envelope and a secure telephone to Washington, sir."

Leland nodded. He picked up his phone. "Maggie, get me

an alpha-one circuit to Washington. Mr. Carter will be using it.'' He handed the phone to Carter. ''When you're finished, I'll be in the outer office with your envelope.''

''I won't be long,'' Carter said. The ambassador left, and within a couple of minutes Carter had his Washington number.

Although it was very early in the morning in Washington, Hawk came on the line almost immediately, his voice particularly gruff. ''You're breaking security.''

''Yes, sir, but I'm going to need some help.''

''Just a moment,'' Hawk said. Carter could almost see the man lighting a cigar and perhaps switching on a tape recorder even though all of his calls, even at home, were automatically recorded at AXE headquarters on Dupont Circle. ''Go ahead, N3.''

Quickly and succinctly, Carter related everything that had happened to him since he had arrived in London scarcely twenty-four hours ago.

''Sounds like you've stirred up a hornets' nest.''

''Yes, sir.''

''It also sounds like Rojas is dealing with some pretty tough people. But we expected that. Were they Russian or Eastern European?''

''Neither, sir,'' Carter said. Hawk was referring to the two men in the study at the Château Le Favre. ''And they weren't Middle Eastern. They seemed English. Or maybe South African.''

''There's a good man there in our London embassy. Lowenstein. He'll be able to work up sketches for you, and we'll take it from there.''

''Thanks, sir. Meanwhile, there's quite a large pile of money in my account at the Ritz.''

''Yes, congratulations. Finance will be happy for a change.''

"It's just that, sir. I'll be needing that money a little longer."

"You have a couple of hundred thousand pounds, from what I understand, plus your credit cards . . ."

"Yes, sir, but I've won a bundle from Rojas. He's going to want it back. All of it."

"Yes?" Hawk said cautiously.

"His people will know if the money is transferred out."

"But we can process it, Nick—"

"It's not that, sir," Carter cut in. "All the money has to be left in sight. We'll meet again. Perhaps I'll lose some, perhaps I'll win some more, but it's got to remain like a carrot in front of the donkey's nose."

"You *will* win, sooner or later."

"Oh, yes, sir. I expect I will. But it has to seem nip and tuck for a while. Or at least the money always has to be in plain sight, for Rojas."

"All right, Nick. I'll keep Finance at bay, although they'll probably howl. When will you be leaving for Germany?"

"Sir?"

"Germany. Baden-Baden. I just got the call twenty minutes ago. Thought that's what you were responding to. Rojas just left London and is on his way to Baden-Baden."

"No, sir, I hadn't known. What hotel?"

"The Brenners Parkhotel."

"Thank you, sir. I'll be leaving within a couple of hours."

"Good luck," Hawk said.

When Carter hung up, he went out to the ambassador waiting in the outer office. The man had a large padded envelope, which he handed over.

Carter quickly addressed the envelope to Rojas in care of the deluxe hotel in Baden-Baden, and then, in front of the wide-eyed secretary and the startled ambassador, he stuffed the two guns and the two wallets inside, and stapled the envelope closed.

"Get this across in the diplomatic pouch, then see that it gets delivered," Carter said.

Leland nodded but said nothing.

SIX

Baden-Baden, an ancient city, was founded by the Roman emperor Hadrian in the second century A.D. It is situated at the edge of the Black Forest and among other things is noted as a health spa because of its hot mineral springs.

Carter wanted Rojas to know he was being chased but didn't want it to be obvious, so he took the boat-train from London to Paris, then the train to Strasbourg. He hired a limousine to take him the final few miles north and across the border to the German city.

But neither Rojas nor Carter had come to Baden-Baden for its springs or its history. Rojas had come because of the casino at which baccarat was featured. And Carter came because he was on the hunt.

Carter managed to sleep for nearly six hours on the trip over, and he was refreshed as he got out of the limo in front of the Parkhotel on Schillerstrasse. The casino was nearby, and the hotel was one of the better in Germany.

He had had the Ritz call ahead for reservations, and inside he was given the VIP treatment. Only his signature and passport were required; everything else had been taken care of for him.

At the desk he had the hotel manager promise to telephone

the casino and make credit arrangements, and then he went upstairs to his suite to dress for the evening.

It was well after six o'clock when Carter had finished in the bathroom. He had nearly finished dressing in his freshly cleaned tuxedo, when room service showed up with a bottle of very good champagne.

"I didn't order this," Carter said.

"No, sir," the room service waiter said, wheeling in the cart. He made a show of opening the wine.

"Complimentary?"

"Actually no, sir. A card comes with it," the waiter said. He handed Carter a card in a small envelope, then poured a glass of the wine. Carter tipped him, and the man left.

The card was written in what was obviously a woman's hand: *Enjoy. From an admirer.*

The champagne was very expensive and very good. Carter lit a cigarette, then telephoned for a reservation at the Schwarwaldgrill restaurant downstairs for eight o'clock.

He turned on some music, then took a glass of champagne out on the terrace. England had been overcast and rainy. Here the weather was cool but clear. The smells from the nearby forest and the park just behind the hotel were sweet. Carter breathed deeply, exhaling slowly.

This assignment was slowly working into something he enjoyed. Later this evening he would challenge Rojas at baccarat, a game that any trained monkey could play . . . any lucky monkey, that is. But it did demand courage, something Carter instinctively felt Rojas lacked. He would have preferred to continue playing poker or even craps, which took a certain amount of skill with percentages. Even roulette, if played correctly, was a game of skill, as was blackjack. But baccarat—or chemin de fer or punto banco, however it was called—demanded nothing more of its players than guts.

Washington, D.C., his apartment, and the embassy cocktail party circuit seemed a long way off at this quiet, contemplative moment. For years, it seemed, he had sat around idly while the world and her real problems passed him by. He had been frustrated during the months of relative inactivity. So frustrated in fact, that he had been worried about going overboard on whatever his next assignment might be.

But now he was beginning to feel comfortable. His old sense of challenge had come back. Rojas was up to something serious. Carter's job was not merely to stop whatever it was, but he had to find out what Rojas was doing, who he was doing it for, and if possible, bend it to America's advantage.

He looked at the card that had come with the champagne. There was only one woman who could possibly know he was here: Carmella Perez.

She had come on to him at the casino in the Ritz and again at the tables in the Alhambra. Was she interested in him? Or did playing cards dangerously just turn her on?

Inside, Carter poured himself another glass of champagne, then tied his bow tie, strapped on Wilhelmina, made sure Hugo and Pierre were in their proper places, then pulled on his jacket.

He sipped at the champagne, then pocketed his lighter and put a dozen cigarettes into his gold cigarette case, which went into a breast pocket.

He finished the glass of wine, then left his room and took the elevator downstairs. He dropped the key off at the desk, then sauntered across to the bar and ordered an Asbach-Urhalt brandy.

"*Guten Abend*, Herr Carter," the barman said. "Your table is ready anytime you wish it."

Carter smiled and inclined his head slightly. The word had spread swiftly. Carter, the high roller from London, was here. No doubt in pursuit of Rojas, the other high roller.

There would undoubtedly be a crowd at the casino this evening. And if the fight continued for another evening, the crowd would be even larger.

It was exactly what Carter wanted. Attention. Not so much that Rojas would run, but enough to make the man very nervous . . . so nervous, in fact, that he'd make mistakes.

He sipped at his brandy, lit another cigarette, then glanced across the bar toward where a trio was setting up for the evening.

"Good evening, Mr. Carter," a woman said behind him.

Without turning he knew who it was. "Senhorita Perez," he said, facing her. He got to his feet. "Slumming?"

She laughed, her voice as lovely as her face. "There must be a different connotation to that term than I am aware of."

"No."

"Then I would say no, I am not slumming. I am doing the opposite." She shook her head. "I am confused. Is such a thing possible?"

Carter smiled and held the barstool for her while she sat. "Sure," he said, taking his own seat. "It's called 'puttin' on the ritz.' "

She laughed again. "That is an old song . . ."

"That's right," Carter said. "I think Fred Astaire sang it in a thirties' movie musical."

The barman came, and Carmella ordered a glass of white wine. Carter finished his brandy and ordered another.

"Thank you for the champagne," Carter said, watching her eyes. They widened slightly.

"Champagne?" she asked innocently.

"It doesn't matter. What brings you here this evening? I thought you would be with Rojas and his entourage."

Their drinks came.

"I have been sent to spy on you. Find out what you are after. Find out who sent you. Find out how it is you are here so soon in Baden-Baden."

"I'm after Rojas's money. My own greed has sent me. And I too had spies back at the Ritz who told me you had come here."

"You intend following Juan along the circuit?"

"Depends upon what the circuit is."

"You know—London, here, Monte Carlo, Las Vegas. The circuit."

"As long as I win and he loses."

"Mr. Carter . . ."

"Nick."

"Nick. Do not do this. It is a foolish mistake. Juan will . . . do something very bad. He must win, you know? He cannot lose."

"Something very bad . . . he'll have me killed?"

"Yes."

"He has had others killed?"

Carmella looked away in frustration for a moment. "I did not come here to have this kind of a conversation with you. I came here to warn you. Do not challenge Juan."

"And your introduction was the champagne?"

"No," she said. "Juan sent it to your room. He told me what to write on the card."

"Then you've discharged your duties," Carter said coldly. He turned away. "You no longer have to remain here. His goons are no doubt watching me."

She reached out and touched his arm. "No, you do not understand, Nick."

He turned to her. "What?"

"It's not that way with . . . me."

Carter said nothing.

She had looked away, but she turned back and looked defiantly into his eyes. "When I first saw you at the Ritz, and then again at the Alhambra, I . . ."

Carter held his silence.

"I was attracted to you."

Carter suddenly felt like a bastard, but this pretty young woman would be a way to get to Rojas. "It's all right . . ." he started.

She picked up her wineglass, took a sip, carefully set the glass back on the bar, and then without warning slapped Carter hard in the face. "Bastard," she hissed. She got off the barstool and stormed out of the lounge.

The barman rushed up. "Is there anything the matter, *mein Herr*?"

"Everything's fine," Carter growled. He threw back his drink, left the bar, and presented himself to the maître d', who seated him immediately.

He ordered another bottle of the champagne Rojas had sent up to his room, a half-dozen oysters on the half shell, soup, salad, and the pheasant.

Throughout the meal, Carter was short with the waiters and the busboys who served him. He was in a savage mood, which he figured was just as well for whatever might happen at the casino that evening. But he was troubled because he could not bring himself to identify the exact nature of his mood. Or the exact cause of it. Although way back inside he knew damned well what had set him off.

He finished the wine and his meal. Afterward, he had coffee and a Rémy, tipped ostentatiously, and left the hotel, walking around the corner to the casino.

The fresh air, rather than calming him down, deepened his black mood, so that by the time he'd paid his way into the *salle privée* of the casino, he was eager to meet Rojas at any game the man preferred and grind him into the floorboards.

To say the casino was ornate was an understatement. Red damask wallpaper competed with brightly lit crystal chandeliers hanging from a heavily molded ceiling in which garish rococo paintings were gilded and back-lit.

Nearly all the men were dressed in tuxedoes, the women in evening dresses and dripping with jewels. Among many of them, there seemed to be a bored indifference to their elegant surroundings. But it was a studied disregard. Carter had seen it before in others who were trying, usually without much success, to be sophisticated.

There were a lot of Arabs in this group, many with Western girl friends. He had noticed the same thing in London. They were the people nowadays who had the real money to spread around.

The *salle privée* was fairly large. Carter did a couple of turns around the room, snagging a glass of champagne from a passing waiter, without spotting Rojas or his group. They were probably still back at the hotel. It was relatively early.

He had had the hotel advance him some cash on his credit account. The actual cash would be coming from London very soon. In the meantime, everyone assured him that his marker would be good here for as much as he wished.

A couple of good-looking older women were seated at the blackjack table. Carter joined them, laying a thousand-mark chip on the square in front of him.

Both women glanced from his face to the chip, their eyes widening slightly. They had been playing with hundred-mark tokens.

Carter's first two cards were a pair of tens. He doubled up his bet, drawing a five on one, another ten on the other. He split the second pair.

One of the ladies had gone bust, but the other held. Carter hit his first pair, drawing a seven for a bust. He drew an ace on one of his tens for blackjack, and a nine on the other.

The dealer went bust, and the woman next to Carter, who had held with what turned out to be sixteen, clapped her hands.

In the next round Carter went bust, so he doubled his bet to two thousand marks.

In the third, fourth, and fifth draws Carter was beat by the dealer, each time doubling his bet, so that by the sixth hand he'd laid out 32,200 marks. A number of people had gathered around the table. Another older woman joined them.

The cards were dealt. The dealer's up card was a ten. Carter drew a pair of fives. It was a pair that was usually never split. The chances of getting a ten—to make twenty—were very good. But the dealer's ten meant that he too had a good chance for twenty.

Carter split his pair, was dealt a ten first out, and a nine for the second five.

The crowd behind him was loving it. Carter was in a tight spot. If he stayed, he lost automatically. If he hit, he had a good chance on both hands of busting.

He scratched for a first hit, which was a six for a three-card twenty-one. The crowd was respectfully silent. He scratched for a hit on the second of the pairs, then drew an ace for fifteen. He grinned and scratched for another hit, drawing a deuce for seventeen. The crowd ate it up.

Carter showed the lady beside him his hand. She clucked and shook her head.

"What will you do, *monsieur*?" she asked.

"I need another card," Carter said, turning back to the dealer.

The card came, and Carter made a great show of looking at it. The crowd gasped. He had drawn a trey for twenty.

The dealer flipped his down card over. It was a nine. He had to stand at nineteen. The crowd applauded as Carter flipped over his cards and collected his 64,400 marks.

"That was very well done, *monsieur*," the French woman next to him said.

Carter got up and tossed the dealer a hundred-mark chip. "*Danke*," he said. He leaned over and pecked the woman on the cheek. "*Merci*."

"For what, you lovely man?"

"For your luck."

The dealer nodded his thank-you, and Carter turned away from the table directly into Rojas, who stood there with two of his goons behind him and one of his young women—not Carmella Perez—beside him.

"You are a very lucky man, Mr. Carter," Rojas said.

Carter's black mood had faded when he gambled, but it came back now. "I would have thought you'd had enough in London."

The atmosphere in the room was suddenly electric. Those who knew or suspected something might occur between Rojas and Carter were watching carefully. The others in the room simply knew something exciting was starting to happen.

Rojas was a study in admirable self-control. "In London we played poker. Your game. Here the specialty is baccarat."

"I beat you at a man's game, why not try a woman's game?" Carter snapped. He started to brush past Rojas, but the businessman stopped him.

"Before we begin, *senhor*, can you tell me what it is you do not like about me? Why are you so obviously out to get me?"

Carter stepped back and looked into the man's eyes. He smiled. "I don't like being waylaid on English country roads."

"I do not know what you are talking about . . ."

"Then you haven't received my package from London

yet?'' Carter asked. ''The one with the wallets and the guns?''

Rojas's eyes went flinty. ''It *was* you.''

''No, *senhor*, it was *your* people. I don't like being manhandled.''

''You were lucky.''

''Yes,'' Carter said. ''Perhaps. Now, do you wish to talk, fight, or play cards?''

Rojas did not say anything for a moment or two. Then only the people nearest them could actually overhear the conversation between Rojas and Carter, but everyone else understood that something dangerous was occurring.

''You are a confident man. Perhaps too confident?''

''As long as I'm not being seriously challenged, I can afford to have a good time,'' Carter said. This time when he stepped by, Rojas made no move to stop him.

Carter walked around the blackjack tables to the two baccarat tables nearest the front entrance to the private room.

One of the tables was already occupied with a half-dozen players. At the other, two Arabs were waiting along with the casino's *observateur*, who sat in his tall chair.

The velvet rope was clipped back, inviting players. Carter stepped up to the table, nodded to the man in the tall chair, then to the Arab gentlemen.

''Permit me to introduce myself . . .'' he began, but the *observateur* motioned him toward a seat.

''That will not be necessary, Herr Carter. We know you.''

Carter sat, lit a cigarette, then ordered a cognac. Rojas showed up a few moments later. He too was recognized, and he sat across the table from Carter.

''Welcome, Herr Rojas,'' the *observateur* said respectfully.

''We are here to play serious baccarat,'' Rojas said pompously. Carter barely suppressed a smile.

"Of course, *mein Herr,*" the man in the tall chair said.

Both Arabs sat up. They had very large piles of markers beside them. They were not shills, Carter decided. But they would provide the impetus for Rojas to bite off as much or more than he could chew. If Rojas did not pick up Carter's bet, the Arabs would. But Carter figured that if he had to, he could coast when Rojas had the bank. It would further anger the man.

Several decks of cards were shuffled and placed in the wooden shoe, which was nothing more than a mechanical dealer. The shoe was offered to Carter, who accepted it.

Carter laid down 25,000 marks in chips, a respectable opening even for this casino.

Rojas immediately covered the bet. "Banquo," he said. The Arabs bet between themselves, which was not strictly legal, but no one stopped them.

Carter deftly flipped the cards out of the shoe, and the croupier, who showed up at the very last moment, used his long-handled paddle to deal them out.

Rojas grinned and flipped his cards over. He was showing a natural nine. Carter had only a six. The croupier shoved Carter's bet across to the Brazilian.

Carter laid down 50,000 marks. Rojas again covered the bet. The two Arabs sat back, fully aware now and respectful of the fact that this was some sort of a personal contest between Rojas and Carter.

Carter dealt the two cards each. Again Rojas flipped his over, this time coming up with a natural eight for a win. Carter had drawn a pair of queens, a zero.

This time he laid out 100,000 marks. Rojas hesitated, a slight grin coming to his lips.

"Is there something the matter?" Carter asked. "Perhaps you wish to drop out so soon, Senhor Rojas?"

"Your rather simple strategy here seems to be the same as

it was at the blackjack table.''

''And that is?''

''Double your bet each time you lose. Sooner or later your luck will change and you will make a killing.''

Carter smiled. ''Simple but effective.''

''But not real gambling.''

''You have a suggestion to make the contest more interesting?''

Rojas inclined his head. ''At the Alhambra you took from me in the neighborhood of three quarters of a million pounds. That is equivalent, more or less, to two and a half million marks. What say to a bet, including what you've won here this evening, of an even three million marks?''

Carter seemed to think about it for a long time. A lot of people had gathered around the table standing silently behind the velvet ropes. The *salle privée* manager came up. Carter looked at him. The man nodded, the movement almost imperceptible. It meant Carter's credit limit was good.

''Very well,'' Carter said. ''An even three million marks.''

SEVEN

It seemed as if most of the activity in the casino had temporarily come to a halt. Word had spread that there was action at a baccarat table. Very big action. Three million marks, after all, was considered to be a major bet in any casino in any country amongst any company. Even the Arabs, whose incomes were annually in the tens of millions, sat back respectfully to watch the North American and the South American go at it.

Three fresh decks were loaded into the shoe, which was passed to Carter.

Carter was brought another cognac, and Rojas a glass of Perrier. There was one good thing about the game of baccarat, Carter thought. As long as you kept your manners, it did not matter if you were drunk or sober. Playing the game demanded only luck, not skill.

Deftly he slapped out the first three cards from the shoe. The croupier discarded them, and slowly, one card at a time, he slipped out two cards each. The croupier passed them.

Rojas eased his cards up so that he could just see their value. A slight smile flickered across his lips. He laid his cards back.

Carter eased his cards up. He too grinned. He had drawn a

king and a five. Possibly the worst combination in baccarat. To make anything out of it would be very difficult.

Rojas sipped his sparkling water.

"Another card, *senhor*?" Carter asked.

Rojas took his time about shaking his head and saying no.

Carter slipped a card out of the shoe for himself, but before he turned it face up as was required, he lit a cigarette and took a sip of his cognac.

"Before we go any further, *senhor*, would you be interested in making the contest more interesting still?" Carter asked.

"You have not shown your draw."

"No."

"You are bluffing. You had a bad hand, perhaps a three or four, and now you are trying to bid me out of the game."

"If you had drawn an eight or a nine, you would not still be talking, *senhor*. And unless I am mistaken, you are a wealthy man for whom a few million marks cannot be so catastrophic."

Rojas's nostrils flared. "What have you in mind?"

"I would like to double the bet."

A gasp went through the crowd. When it was over, there wasn't a sound in the *salle privée*.

"To six million marks?" the croupier asked.

"If Senhor Rojas is interested," Carter said.

After a moment one of the Arabs sat forward. "If the gentleman is not interested, I would be happy to pick up the three million. You are lucky, Mr. Carter, but not *that* lucky."

"That won't be necessary," Rojas said. The *observateur* nodded to Rojas, extending his limit. Rojas turned back. "The bet is six million marks."

Carter smiled, finished his cognac, and turned his cards over one by one, starting with the king for zero, then the five, leaving his last card still down.

Rojas was grinning broadly. The Arabs were smiling too. The crowd held its breath. Rojas did not have an eight or a nine, otherwise he would have declared his natural. The way he was smiling meant he probably had a seven.

"You have one more card," Rojas said.

"So I do," Carter agreed. He flipped the card over. There was a gasp followed by pandemonium as everyone realized that he had turned over a four, for a total of nine. No matter what Rojas had, Carter was the winner.

Rojas was livid. On a signal from the *observateur*, the casino's security people moved in around the South American's bodyguards, who were shaking like the big cats in a zoo at feeding time.

Carter sat back, calmly smoking, and looked into Rojas's eyes. The Brazilian, the tremendous effort visible on his face, forced himself to calm down.

"Another game, *senhor*?" Carter asked.

A sudden hush fell over the crowd.

Rojas slowly shook his head. "Not this evening, I think. My luck cannot stand up to such an onslaught as yours."

Carter inclined his head, shoved his chair back, and stood up. He made no move to touch the huge pile of oblong markers in front of him on the table. That would have been very bad form.

"I think ten percent would be an appropriate thank-you to the casino. I don't need the cash in any event," Carter said haughtily. The *observateur* nodded his thanks on behalf of the casino and the velvet rope was pulled back.

Four of the casino's security men immediately fell in behind Carter and escorted him slowly across the *salle privée*, down the stairs, across the main entry hall, and outside.

"May we suggest a car to your hotel, Herr Carter?" one of

the security men asked.

"By all means," Carter said.

He climbed into the back seat of the huge Mercedes 600 that slid up the driveway, and within a couple of minutes he was being deposited at the hotel.

Carter watched the car leave, then he went into the hotel, got his key, and took the elevator up to his suite.

He was tired. It was a combination of the excitement, the danger, and some jet lag that was finally catching up with him, as well as the drinks he had had this evening.

The lights were on low, and music was playing from the stereo when he opened the door to his suite. Immediately he fell back, pulling out his Luger.

For several long moments he stood there in a half crouch in the doorway. Cautiously he eased himself inside, shut the door behind him, and carefully made his way down the short corridor and into the main sitting room.

A bottle of champagne and two glasses had been set up in an ice bucket on the sideboard. Only one light was on. The stereo was playing something that sounded like Mozart, and the door to the bedroom was open, a light shining from within.

This smacked of Rojas's touch. But how had he gotten his people up here so quickly? It didn't make a lot of sense. Unless he had contemplated losing. . . .

Across the large sitting room, Carter flattened himself against the wall beside the bedroom door and carefully looked inside. The bed had been turned down, the door to the bathroom was open, and he could hear someone singing. It was a woman.

Carter went into the bedroom—a round in the Luger's firing chamber, the safety off—and crossed to the bathroom door.

Carmella Perez lay soaking in the large tub, the whirlpool

jets on, her eyes closed as she hummed a little tune. There were no soap bubbles, only the circulating water swirling around her lovely body.

Carter watched her for a moment, admiring her slender legs, her elegant neck, and her ample breasts. She was a beautiful woman, but she was trouble of a different sort with Rojas. Gambling was bad enough. Women and gambling were an explosive combination.

Later, he told himself. If he had to, he would use this woman to hit Rojas even harder. But for now he did not need the complication.

"Time to leave, Senhorita Perez," Carter said, holstering his Luger and stepping across the bathroom.

Carmella opened her eyes, looked up, and smiled, her moist lips parted, her perfect white teeth gleaming.

Her smile died as Carter reached down into the tub, released the drain, and shut off the whirlpool.

"What . . . ?" she sputtered.

He turned, got a large bath towel from the rack, and held it out to her. "Time to go back to your boss. I'm afraid he will be in great need of comforting this evening."

Carmella just looked up at him for a long time, then she shook her head. "You and he gambled?"

Carter nodded.

"You won?"

Carter grinned. "Six million marks. At his own game, too."

"*Deus*," she said softly. She stood up, the halo around her nipples very dark, as was the small tuft of hair at her pubis. Her complexion was tawny and flawless.

Carter held the towel for her, and she stepped out of the tub into it, hugging it closely. She had pinned her hair up, exposing the back of her neck. She looked up into Carter's eyes. She smelled wonderful. At that moment he was very tempted to say the hell with it and take her into his arms.

Instead he turned and went back into the bedroom. Her clothing was tossed over a chair. She followed him out.

"Please do not make me go like this," she said.

"It will be for the best."

"I am sorry for . . . downstairs."

"What do you mean?"

"For in the bar . . . for slapping you. I thought you meant to use me to get at Juan."

"I had considered it," Carter admitted.

Her eyes widened. "But not now?"

"I didn't say that."

"You bastard . . ." she started, but she cut it off. "Are you serious? Did you truly beat him in the casino? Six million marks?"

Carter nodded. "I've told you the truth, now you tell me what you're doing here in my suite."

Carmella was clearly very worried. "I came to seduce you," she said offhandedly.

"Obviously," Carter said dryly. "Did Rojas send you?"

She shook her head. "No. If he knew I was here now like this, he would surely kill me. Especially now that you have hurt him again." She looked at him. "He is certain you are working for the CIA."

Carter opened his mouth to speak, as if he were shocked. But then he threw his head back and laughed out loud. "The CIA?" he said and roared. "That's rich! The stupid bastard gets beaten by a gambler, and immediately he thinks it's some nefarious plot by the American government!"

Carmella was watching him intently, Carter noticed between guffaws. Was the look in her eyes a little too shrewd?

"I came to gamble. It's what I do. And I am very good at it. I've been around gaming tables for most of my life. I understand the people. I understand how to take care of myself. And now it's time for you to go. Get dressed."

"And if I don't go?"

"I'll call Rojas and ask him to come fetch you," Carter snapped. He turned on his heel and went back through the bedroom and into the living room, where he poured himself a glass of champagne.

He shrugged off his jacket, laying it over a chair, undid his tie and top button, and slipped out of his shoulder holster, making sure the safety was on. He laid the Luger aside and went to the window, where he looked outside.

The sky was clear, but it looked cold. It wouldn't be too terribly long before there was snow here, he thought. Perhaps when this was over, he'd take his vacation somewhere in Switzerland, or perhaps Austria. He hadn't been skiing in a long time.

One part of him felt sorry for Carmella Perez. The other part of him, however, the part that didn't quite buy her story that she was here of her own free will, was wary.

He heard her behind him, pouring herself a glass of champagne. In the windowpane he could see her reflection. She had slipped on one of his dress shirts. She wore nothing else, as far as he could see.

For a moment she lingered by his Luger. She reached out and touched the elastic strap of the shoulder holster. When she looked up she didn't seem quite so sure of herself as she had been when she walked into the room.

Carter turned around. "I thought I told you to get dressed and get out of here."

"Do you always carry a gun?"

"When I'm doing any serious gambling, yes. Especially when I'm gambling with men like your boss."

"We have not heard of you."

"Heavy losers usually don't advertise those who beat them."

"You always win?" she asked, a slightly amused expression on her face.

"I make it my business to win. Always."

"Juan will kill you if you continue. Perhaps it is already too late."

"And you will help him?"

She shook her head. "I warned you earlier this evening, and I am here now to warn you again. Get out of Baden-Baden. Leave Juan alone. He is a dangerous man. He too always wins."

"What about you, Carmella? Do you always win?"

"I came here to be with you."

"And afterward?"

"You will leave, and I shall return to Juan." Her lips were moist. Her eyes sparkled. Carter figured his earlier assessment of her, that she simply enjoyed danger, was probably very close to the truth. And yet there was an element to her, something undefinable, that bothered him.

She came languidly across the room, sipping her champagne as she walked.

"I may not leave Baden-Baden after all," Carter said, making no move to reach out for her. She stopped just inches away from him. She had put on some perfume, its scent light and very lovely.

"You say you are a gambler, Nick. You have gotten what you came for. Leave now, in the morning, before it is too late."

Carter smiled. "You said before it might already be too late."

She put down her glass, reached out, and began undoing Carter's shirt studs. He made no move either to aid or hinder her. She ran her hands up his chest, then pulled his head down so that she could kiss him, her tongue brushing his lips.

She looked up into his eyes. "That does not excite you? Perhaps you do not like women . . ."

Carter grinned. He put down his champagne, gathered Carmella in his arms, and kissed her deeply, holding her close against his body, feeling her breasts through the thin shirt material.

When they parted she was flushed.

"You are skilled at other things besides gambling," she whispered.

Carter stepped past her and went to where he had left Wilhelmina. He picked up the Luger and turned back to Carmella. Her eyes were wide.

"Will you shoot me then?"

He said nothing. Instead he took the clip out of the gun, then ejected the single live round from the chamber, which he pocketed. He turned and went into his bedroom, where he got undressed. He shoved the ammunition and his weapons under the bed on his side, first making certain that Carmella was not watching from the doorway. Then he went into the bathroom, turned on the shower, and stepped under the water.

The spray felt wonderful on his tired, tense body, and for the first few moments he willed himself not to think about anything except the moment. But the thought intruded that it was unlikely Rojas would remain in Baden-Baden after his humiliating defeat in the casino.

Carter grinned. When he was on the hunt, his blood flowed and his senses seemed to take on a new sharpness, a heightened sensitivity.

The shower curtains were shoved back and Carmella, again nude, stepped in with Carter.

Without a word she took the soap from him and began lathering his entire body, working from the top down, moving slowly, her hands easing the aches from his sore muscles, lingering here and there when she encountered pronounced scar tissue.

He finally pulled her to her feet, and their slippery bodies came together. This was all a setup, Carter thought. Either that, or she was out for kicks. Either way it was dangerous as hell. But at that moment he found he didn't give a damn. She was a desirable woman. When it was over he would take the consequences.

He kissed her, his hands running down her back to the roundness of her buttocks. She leaned back and looked up at him.

"You are a particularly beautiful man," she murmured. Her half-closed eyes were filled with longing.

The water beat down on them both. Carter slowly turned around, carrying the girl with him, the hard spray rinsing them off. Finally Carter reached out and shoved aside the shower curtains, then reached back and turned off the water.

Carmella's eyes had been closed. She opened them and looked up.

Carter brushed his lips against hers, cutting off what she was about to say, then he reached down and picked her up, and stepped out of the shower.

A warm glow came off her body, and yet she was shivering in Carter's arms. She kept wetting her lips, and her breath was coming rapidly as he carried her out of the bathroom.

He placed her on the king-size bed in the middle of the large bedroom, and slowly he kissed her forehead, her nose, her cheeks, her lips, her chin, her neck.

She arched her back and moaned. Her nipples were erect, and she was already nearly dry from the shower.

"Nick . . ." she breathed.

He kissed her breasts, taking her nipples between his teeth and biting gently as he ran his fingertips slowly along her flanks. Her entire body vibrated like a plucked guitar string.

Carefully his lips worked their way between her breasts and down her stomach to her gently rounded belly, her hips coming up to meet him.

Her legs spread for him as he went lower, kissing the insides of her thighs and the backs of her knees. Every time he touched her with his lips, or his tongue, or his fingertips, she jerked as if receiving electric shocks.

He rose up and brushed his forefinger between her legs, and she gasped in pleasure, her entire body going rigid for one tense moment.

Her eyes were tightly closed, her tongue flicking in and out as she reached down and held his head in her hands.

"Oh, Nick," she breathed again. "*Mãe do Deus*, touch me again . . ."

He lowered himself, his tongue finding her, and she cried out.

Suddenly he rose up and entered her, thrusting deeply into her quivering body.

She was very good, her long, lovely legs wrapped high around his middle as she drew him deeper and deeper in perfect rhythm with her needs as well as his.

And then they were both at the end, holding each other tightly, pushing harder and harder, the almost unbearable pleasure continuing in waves, their bodies totally in tune with one another.

Gradually their movements subsided, punctuated by moments of shivering, intense sensation, until they lay spent in each other's arms.

Slowly Carter became aware of his surroundings. Carmella's eyes were open. She was looking up at him. Smiling.

For a long moment Carter just looked down at her, feeling her body against his, feeling her breasts against his chest, feeling her moistness still surrounding him. But then he noticed a slight glint of triumph in her eyes, and he pushed away, rolling over.

Two of Rojas's goons stood in the doorway, their guns drawn. They were grinning.

Carter relaxed. He glanced over at Carmella, who had shrunk away. It *had* been a setup.

EIGHT

Carmella got dressed and left immediately, but Carter was allowed to clean up. Rojas's men had found his Luger in the sitting room, but as far as they knew, it was the only weapon he possessed.

"Hurry, *senhor*," one of them said as Carter emerged from the bathroom.

"So your boss is mad that I beat him at cards," Carter said, crossing the room and sitting on the edge of the bed. He pulled on his socks. The men were on the other side of the room, watching him. He bent down for his shoe, scooped up his stiletto from beneath the bed, and shoved it, haft-end first, inside his left sock. He quickly slipped on his shoes and stood up.

Carter put on his jacket, and one of Rojas's men quickly frisked him, finding nothing.

Together they left the suite and took the elevator up to the penthouse. Neither of the goons said a thing. They were both very large men, at least six-four and 250 pounds.

"It must be a real interesting job," Carter said to them as they were riding up.

One of them looked at him but said nothing.

"I mean, traveling around the world with Rojas, seeing all those gorgeous women, seeing all the booze and the gambling . . . and not being able to touch one bit of it.''

"Shut up, or I will break your arm,'' one of them said.

Carter chuckled. "Anytime you'd like to try it, pal, just say the word.''

The elevator doors opened, and they went down the broad, tastefully decorated corridor to a huge set of double doors. One of the gorillas rang the doorbell.

The doors opened a second later, and Carter was hustled inside the large, richly furnished penthouse.

Rojas sat at the bar in front of a vast expanse of glass that overlooked the casino. A half-dozen more bodyguards were with him in the main sitting room. One of his women lounged on a long couch.

"Ah, Mr. Carter, I'm so glad you could join me,'' Rojas said.

Carter crossed the room to him. "Up here counting your losses?''

Rojas smiled indulgently. "Let me see, it's cognac you enjoy, is that not correct?''

Carter nodded and sat next to the South American at the bar. The barman poured him a healthy measure of a very old French cognac in a snifter.

Rojas nodded for the man to leave.

"Evidently you did receive my little package,'' Carter said, sipping his drink.

"Package . . .?'' Rojas started to ask, but then recognition dawned in his eyes. "It was you after all who sent me the guns and the wallets. You were not simply playing a little joke.''

Carter nodded.

"Whatever for? They do not belong to me or to any of my

people. Besides, where did you get them?''

"I found them in a trash heap on the road near the Alhambra. If they're not yours, I suggest you turn them over to the police. People so inept that they'd lose their weapons like that shouldn't be allowed to carry them in the first place. Don't you agree?''

Carter could almost hear Rojas's goons in the background grinding their teeth. The woman on the couch giggled.

Rojas turned around to her, a forced smile on his lips. "It is time for you to leave, my dear.''

The girl sat up, a pout on her round face that changed to fear when she realized what kind of a mood her boss was in. She jumped up without a word, and left.

Behind the bar was a large mirror. In it Carter could see the reflected image of the entire sitting room. Two of Rojas's bodyguards were stationed by the door. The other four were positioned around the room. None of them was relaxing. They were all ready for whatever might occur.

Carter didn't think they'd be so brazen as to fire their guns here in the hotel. The two who had come for him carried big .357 magnums without silencers.

With his stiletto in his sock, Carter figured if worse came to worst he could hold Rojas hostage until his people backed down, giving him enough room to get out.

"How is your drink?" Rojas asked, turning back.

"You didn't have me brought up here to feed me good cognac. You're mad that I beat you at the casino.''

"You cheated.''

Carter almost climbed all over the Brazilian, but one of the bodyguards was on him, pinning his arms back. Carter had to play the role, otherwise Rojas would be less inclined to believe he was the professional gambler he claimed to be.

Slowly Carter let himself fall back, willing his muscles to

relax. Rojas finally nodded, and the bodyguard released his grip. Carter straightened up, adjusted his clothing, and took a deep drink of his cognac.

"I never cheat, Rojas," he said. "I don't have to with gamblers like you."

"What do you mean by that?"

"You're a poor gambler. You're an amateur."

"I have had my share of luck, until you."

"You've not gambled against a professional. You've probably played against bored playboys, perhaps rich widows who don't know any better, and of course oil-rich Arabs, most of whom have more money than sense when it comes to things like this."

Rojas just stared at him, a thoughtful expression in his eyes.

Carter glanced at the bodyguards, who were all very alert now.

"That, and the fact that you surround yourself with yes men. There isn't one person here who could tell you the truth if you didn't like it."

"What sort of truth?"

"That you're a fool," Carter said, tensing for an attack.

Rojas went white. It took him almost a minute to regain enough control so that he could speak. There was pure hatred in his eyes. "I called you up here, Mr. Carter, to see if I could talk some sense into you. There is no room for a man such as yourself on the amateur gambling circuit."

"Are you threatening me?"

"Yes, I am," Rojas said. He got off his barstool. "Just so there will be no misunderstanding, I want you to understand that tomorrow I shall be leaving for Monte Carlo. Some old friends will be there, and I shall be playing at the casino. I wouldn't want to see you show up there. You would most certainly get hurt. Badly."

"What does all this mean to you, Rojas?" Carter snapped. "I'm a professional gambler. This is how I make my living. You're rich. What difference does it make to you? Unless . . ." Carter let it trail off. But he was watching Rojas's eyes very carefully. At that last word, the man flinched. Carter had hit a nerve.

"Unless what, Mr. Carter?" Rojas asked softly.

"Unless you aren't so rich. Unless you're in need of some untraceable cash for some reason."

Rojas came very close to Carter. He had a slight odor of cinnamon. His breathing was rapid, and his fists were clenched.

"Get away from me, Carter. Or, as I said, you will most certainly get hurt."

Carter shrugged. Rojas turned and left the room. One of the bodyguards opened the main doors out to the corridor, and the others stepped aside.

Slowly Carter got off his barstool. This was not what he had expected at all. It made him nervous. Rojas had not held him, had not demanded his money be returned, nor had anything been said about Carmella.

Carter reached back for his drink, but the goon next to him batted his hand away. "Get out of here before we decide to take you apart."

Carter looked up at him, then nodded and headed for the door. It wouldn't take much, he figured, to set these guys off. But that would come later, he decided. The odds were a bit lopsided at the moment.

There had not been an elevator operator on the way up. There was one now, however. Carter knew that something would be happening tonight. If any investigation by the local authorities were to be conducted, the elevator operator would swear that he brought the American gentleman down from Rojas's floor in one piece.

The elevator lurched to a halt halfway down to Carter's floor. The operator, an older man, was profusely apologetic. He got on the house phone, and within five minutes they were moving again.

This was a setup. Every nerve in Carter's body knew it was a setup. Yet he could not just turn and walk away from it. He was going to have to continue to beat Rojas at his own game.

He got off the elevator at his floor, and the car continued down.

The door to his suite was slightly ajar. He approached cautiously and shoved the door the rest of the way open with the toe of his shoe. The suite was lit up. Even from the doorway, Carter could see that the place had been ransacked.

He started to bend down for his knife, when the cool barrel of a gun touched the back of his head.

"I would like to blow your brains all over the floor, but that would make such a mess," someone said.

Carter carefully straightened up and stepped inside his suite. Three of Rojas's men were there.

"Did you find what you were looking for?" Carter asked.

"There's no money here beyond a few thousand marks," one of them said in Portuguese.

"I told you—it would be in the hotel safe," the one behind Carter snapped.

"But I did find this," the third one said, holding up Carter's gas bomb, his thumb on the tiny triggering stud.

"I suggest you put that down, or you'll end up killing us all," Carter said in perfect Brazilian Portuguese.

The one holding Pierre laughed and held the bomb up. Carter shrank back, feigning fear. "Jesus Christ," he swore.

The goon holding the bomb suddenly wasn't so sure of himself. "What is this thing?" he asked.

"It's a bomb, you stupid bastard," Carter shouted.

The goon laughed a little. "It isn't so big. Maybe just a firecracker?"

"Play with the trigger much longer and you'll find out just what kind of a firecracker it is."

"Put the thing down, Alejo," the goon behind Carter ordered.

The bodyguard did as he was told, and Carter was prodded across the room, where he was forced to sit down at the desk.

"There is a lot of money downstairs in the hotel safe that is under your control, *senhor*. I want it."

"For Rojas," Carter said, mispronouncing the name.

"I don't know any Rojas," the goon said, pronouncing the name correctly.

Carter laughed. The bodyguard lashed out, the barrel of his big pistol catching Carter in the forehead, just above his hairline.

The other bodyguard was right there, his .357 pressed against Carter's temple.

A trickle of blood ran down Carter's forehead.

"This is most serious, *senhor*. There is no humor in the situation. We wish to have that money. All of it."

"Sure." Carter said, his blood simmering. "Just let me go, and I'll pop downstairs and get it in a big paper bag for you, you dumb son of a bitch."

The pistol whipped around a second time, this time the gunsight opening a long gash across the side of Carter's head, but again it was above the hairline so that no mark would be visible.

Carter gripped the arms of the chair so hard that the wood cracked. Blood streamed down the side of his head, which felt as if it were exploding, and his vision blurred for a few moments before it finally cleared.

One of the other goons had laid something on the table. He

shoved Carter around to the desk.

"This is a draft on your account downstairs. It is in the amount of ten million marks. We know you have that much."

"You want me to sign this ridiculous piece of paper?"

The big man raised his heavy pistol to strike out again. But Carter looked up and snapped, "If you hit me with that again, buddy, you'd better kill me, because I will surely cut off your *cajones* and stuff them down your throat so that you will choke to death."

The goon hesitated, the pistol over his head. Carter stared at him for a long time, then turned away.

"You'd better find out from your boss just how far you can go," he said calmly. His head was splitting.

"You will sign this!" one of the men ordered.

"No," Carter said, "I will not sign this. Nor would you want me to."

Again a .357 was pressed against his temple. The hammer was cocked, the sound very loud so close to his ear. "It is time to finish with this little game, *senhor*," the goon said. "Sign the draft or you will die."

"Fuck you," Carter said. He knew he was playing an exceedingly dangerous game, but he did not think Rojas had ordered his people to kill him. Later Rojas probably would, but not here in the hotel and not like this. Too many questions would be raised. Too many fingers would most certainly be pointed back at Rojas.

There had certainly been plenty of antagonism between the two men. Gamblers in two casinos in two countries had seen the instant bad blood between Carter and Rojas.

Such hard feelings could conceivably justify roughing up Carter. But nothing could justify murder.

"What will we do?" one of them asked in Portuguese.

"Shut up, you silly bastard, and let me think!"

The other one shoved the man holding the pistol against Carter's head aside, and Carter looked up in time to see a right hook coming at his face.

He just managed to pull his head to the left and fall back with the blow, yet he was knocked backward with the force of the punch.

Feigning grogginess, Carter just lay where he fell until the one who had hit him bent down over him. Carter reached up and grabbed the man by the throat, his powerful fingers crushing the goon's windpipe while he wrapped his legs around the man's back, holding him in place.

"Alejo! What is it?" one of the others shouted.

A line of spittle dribbled from the man's mouth as his tongue came out, and his eyes finally rolled up into his head.

Carter let go as one of the other men grabbed his companion and pulled the body aside. In that moment Carter had slipped out his stiletto, and he rose up like an angry bear from its den, burying Hugo's blade to its haft in the man's chest, then yanking the blade to the left between two ribs with every ounce of his strength.

A gush of blood spurted from the man's chest as Carter heaved him upward toward the final bodyguard, who had drawn his gun. The man fired once, hitting the dead body of his partner, as Carter kicked out and knocked him off his feet.

"Son of a bitch," the thug swore.

Carter was on him, breaking his arm as his gun hand came up, the bone snapping with an audible crack.

Just as the bodyguard was about to scream with pain and fear, Carter reached up and covered his nose and mouth with one hand. Using his other hand as a fulcrum, he pushed backward.

The goon's legs bucked, his entire body heaved, and he voided in his trousers the moment his neck broke, a powerful stench filling the air.

Carter rolled aside, his stomach churning, and he got shakily to his feet. His vision kept going out of focus, and he was covered with blood, his own as well as from the gorilla in whose chest Hugo's blade was still lodged.

The bodyguard with the broken neck was still kicking and squirming. Finally he stopped, his entire body stiff.

For a minute or two, Carter just leaned back against the edge of the couch, catching his breath and wiping the blood from his eyes.

Carter had known this was coming, so he was not surprised. On the contrary, he was angry.

"Push Rojas," his instructions read. Push the man to the limit. He'll break.

Carter shoved himself away from the couch, then stumbled to the door and locked it, making sure the chain was in place. Then he went into his bathroom and took a long, hot shower, followed by an icy cold spray, the bleeding from his scalp wounds finally slowing down. But his vision remained the same, going in and out of focus at the odd moment.

He dried himself, got dressed in clean clothing, and felt much better when he went back out into the carnage of his sitting room.

The entire suite stank of death. Carter pulled the stiletto out of the man's chest, cleaned it off in the bathroom, then strapped it onto his right forearm beneath his shirt sleeve in its chamois sheath. He donned his gas bomb, and in his bedroom, hung over a chair, was his Luger in its shoulder holster. They had brought it back.

As he strapped on Wilhelmina's reassuring bulk, he understood that once he had signed the draft, they *had* meant to kill him. Otherwise they would not have brought his gun back to him.

Operations wanted Rojas stopped. But more importantly they wanted to know what the man was up to. Who he was working for. What kind of mischief he would inflict on the Caribbean basin.

At this moment, however, Carter felt he didn't give a damn what his instructions were. Rojas had struck out at him. The arrogant bastard had been so self-assured that he had struck right here in the very hotel in which he was staying. Rojas felt he was above the law and even above retribution.

Once again in the sitting room, Carter telephoned Rojas's suite. The phone rang a half-dozen times before Carter got the hotel operator on the line.

"I'm trying to reach Senhor Rojas," he said, "but there is no answer."

"Herr Rojas and his party checked out just a few minutes ago, *mein Herr*."

"Checked out?" Carter repeated dumbly.

"*Ja, mein Herr*. Would you care to forward a message?"

"What hotel is he going to?"

"The Hôtel de Paris in Monte Carlo. Do you wish to forward a message?"

"No, that's not necessary," Carter said, and he hung up.

He lit a cigarette, then poured a drink from the sideboard. Rojas had evidently come back from the casino, had checked out, and then just before he left had brought Carter up to his penthouse suite for their little tête-à-tête.

Carter had an almost overwhelming urge to race out of his suite, commandeer a car, and hurry out to the airport to intercept the bastard.

He looked around the sitting room. All hell would break loose unless this mess was cleaned up. If the hotel staff came in and discovered what had gone on here, the German authorities would arrest him, and then there'd be a lot of difficult explanations that would almost certainly tip Rojas off that Carter was much more than a lucky, tough gambler.

Quickly he went through the three dead men's pockets, but

he came up with nothing more than he had expected: the usual innocuous IDs, a few marks in loose change, some odds and ends.

Someone knocked at the door just as he was finishing.

Carter spun around, his Luger in his hand, a shell in the firing chamber almost before he realized what he had done. He hurried across the room to the door and put his ear to the wood.

It was very quiet for a long time, until whoever it was outside decided to knock again. There was no peephole in the door.

"Nick? It is Carmella."

Carter opened the door for her, his Luger at the ready. She was alone, and she appeared to be very frightened.

He pulled her inside. "What are you doing here?" he demanded roughly.

Her eyes went wide as she surveyed the shambles and finally saw the three dead men. Her hands went to her mouth.

"*Mãe do Deus*," she whispered.

"What are you doing back here?" Carter asked again. "Rojas has checked out, I'm told."

Carmella looked up at him. "Yes, he is on the way to the airport. We are going to Monte Carlo."

"So what are you doing here?"

She looked at the dead men. "Juan said I was to ride back with . . . Alejo and his people. He said I was to come down here first, though, and explain to you that we could not see each other again."

"The sadistic bastard," Carter said half under his breath. Rojas had meant for Carmella to come down here and see his body. Her punishment for having so enjoyed her infidelity.

NINE

"I don't know what to do," Carmella said. She refused to move away from the doorway and step into the suite.

"You set this up, so you shouldn't be so squeamish," Carter snapped. He was having trouble figuring out just how he felt about her.

She looked up at him with her dark, liquid eyes. "Juan made me do it. He would have killed me." She looked again at the three dead men. "But now . . . I don't know what to do, or where to go."

Carter shook his head. "Take a cab out to the airport. If you don't get there in time to catch your boss, then take the next commercial flight out."

"But what shall I tell him?"

"Tell him that when you came here to my room, it was empty. You didn't see me or the other three."

"What will you do with . . . ?"

"I'll have it taken care of. There is someone here in this hotel who owes me a favor."

Carmella was shivering. She came into Carter's arms. "Hold me, please," she said in a very small voice.

Carter held her. She was a very complicated woman. Lost, he suspected, in Rojas's spell of power. Somehow she had fallen into his circle, and now it was too late for her to extricate herself. She knew it, and it frightened her.

She was crying. When they parted, Carter kissed her.

"We will not be seeing each other again . . ." she started, but then her eyes widened. She shook her head in disbelief. She had read something in Carter's eyes. "You are planning on coming to Monte Carlo?"

"Yes."

"That is insanity! He will kill you for sure!"

"I don't think so. Or at least it will not be as easy as he first suspected."

"You mean to gamble with him?"

"I mean to run him into the ground."

Carmella backed away, reaching out for the door handle. "You are crazy. You will be a dead man."

Carter smiled. "But I will see you in Monte Carlo."

"Crazy," she said again. She pulled open the door and hurried down the corridor without looking back.

Carter watched until she took the elevator down, then he closed and locked the door, and telephoned his contact man for Germany in Berlin. Rojas was gone, and as far as he was concerned, Carter no longer posed a threat. So it wasn't likely he still had anyone on the hotel staff watching. There would be no need for it.

"Amalgamated Press," a singsong female voice answered.

"This is Carter. Patch me over to the chief of station."

"Yes, sir," the woman said. Within a few seconds the connection was made. Considering the hour, Carter figured the man was at home.

"Yes," a sleepy voice answered.

"Do you know where I am?"

"Yes." The voice was suddenly wide awake.

"I am leaving soon. But first there is a housekeeping chore that I will need help with. Here in my room."

"How many of them?" the chief of station asked. He understood exactly what Carter was saying. This had happened before.

"Three. Have you someone here who can be trusted?"

"Yes. It will be perhaps a half hour. You will wait there?"

"Yes."

The connection was broken, and Carter hung up the telephone. Peter Bream was the man's name. Carter had known him briefly during the man's Washington stint. He was German, and he was very good at his job, very precise.

It took almost an hour for the two men Bream had called to show up. While he waited, Carter packed his bags, stowing his weapons in the cassette recorder. He telephoned the desk and found out that the next plane to Nice would not be until tomorrow morning, but he could make the train, which would place him in Monte Carlo by morning.

He ordered a cab to get him to the train station in Strasbourg and asked the desk to make his reservations at the Hôtel de Paris. He also asked that his funds be transferred to the hotel.

He put his bags out in the corridor for the bellmen to take downstairs.

Five minutes later Bream's two men showed up. Carter let them in. They were dressed in evening clothes so they would attract no attention. They were both very large, and looked a lot like Rojas's goons.

"You are checking out now?" one of them asked. The other was poking around the room, surveying the damage.

"My bags are already downstairs. A cab is waiting. I'm taking the night train to Nice."

"From Strasbourg?"

Carter nodded. "Will you have any trouble here, with this?"

"None at all, sir," the other man said. "Have a good trip."

"It's essential that this be handled quietly."

"Of course," one of them said.

Bream was sharp; he would not have sent amateurs. They would handle this with no problem. By the time the chambermaid came in the morning, the room would look as if nothing had happened.

Downstairs, Carter settled his bill, then signed the draft order so that his funds, which amounted to something over ten million marks, would be transferred.

There was some sort of a mix-up with the draft order, so it took nearly ten minutes before it was actually completed.

As he was leaving the desk to go outside to his waiting cab, Carter just caught a glimpse of two men dressed in hotel maintenance uniforms stepping off an elevator. They were pushing a large laundry cart. One of them glanced toward Carter. He was one of Bream's people.

Carter's step was much lighter as he hurried outside and climbed into the back seat of his cab. If word of what happened had gotten back to Rojas, it would make things that much more difficult in Monte Carlo. As far as Rojas was concerned, Carter was still nothing more than a very good gambler out for some kind of dangerous sport. If, however, the Brazilian found out that Carter had had help here, he would know that something bigger was afoot. Presumably he would go to ground at that point, cancelling Carter's mission. It was a delicate situation.

Carter made his train with a half hour to spare. As soon as he was alone in his private compartment, he retrieved his weapons from their hiding place in the recorder, then latched the door, shut out the light, and went to bed.

Monte Carlo would be difficult, he figured. He'd need to be at his best.

As he fell asleep, however, he kept seeing the two men to whom Rojas handed over the attaché case full of money in the Château Le Favre. They were so familiar to him . . . not their faces, but their types. He had given their descriptions to Lowenstein at the U.S. embassy, and the artist had come up with reasonable likenesses. Yet something kept nagging at the back of Carter's consciousness concerning them. Something he felt he should have known.

It was a few minutes before eight on a brilliantly sunny morning when Carter got off the train at Nice and had his bags piled in the rear of a rented Jaguar sedan.

He took his time driving up the E1 to Monaco, enjoying the magnificent scenery and contemplating his next moves against Rojas.

The South American would be surprised when Carter showed up. Hopefully he'd be off-balance enough to make some blunder that would reveal his plans, or at least give some indication as to what he was up to.

If the man was planning something for the Caribbean, he would not be doing it alone. He'd have to have help.

The only thing Carter could figure was that Rojas was making a lot of noise on the gambling circuit as a cover for his real activities. He evidently was meeting with his associates.

One fact did not fit that neat assessment, however, and it bothered Carter. Why had Rojas handed over money to the two men outside London?

He was paying them off. But for what? To do what? Merely to help him cheat at the casinos? Carter doubted that, although he had been certain that the young dealer at the

Alhambra had been on Rojas's payroll. He did not think the pair at the estate outside Barnet were casino dealers. They simply did not have the look. To Carter they looked more like soldiers than anything else.

That did not fit either, he thought. If there was going to be trouble in the Caribbean and soldiers were to be involved, they'd most likely be Cuban troops, or perhaps even Soviet. The two men at the Château Le Favre were neither.

There was a lot of traffic along the Corniche Inférieure when he drove into the city, and it took him a while to make it around the Port de Fontvieille and the Port de Monaco over to the hotel just diagonally across from the casino.

The doorman, resplendent in an ornate uniform, arranged to have Carter's car parked and his bags brought up to his suite.

Inside, Carter crossed to the front desk, and the hotel manager himself came around and shook his hand.

"Welcome, Monsieur Carter, to the Hôtel de Paris. I hope you had a pleasant journey from Baden-Baden."

"Tolerable," Carter said languidly. "Have there been any messages for me?"

"*Non, monsieur*. Do you wish to see your suite now? We've prepared a light brunch for you."

"How very thoughtful," Carter said. "But first I would like to leave a message for one of your other guests."

"Of course."

"Tell Senhor Rojas that I have arrived and would be delighted to meet him this evening for dinner at the casino."

"*Naturellement*," the manager said. Two bellmen came into the lobby with Carter's bags, and Carter and the manager followed them up to the suite on the fourth floor at the front part of the hotel.

The rooms were huge, furnished with exquisite period pieces and fine carpets. In the bedroom was a large canopied bed. The windows looked down on the casino and on the Place du Casino with its palm trees and other Mediterranean foliage.

"We hope this suite will prove satisfactory, *monsieur*," the manager said without a hint of obsequiousness. After all, he was the manager of Monte Carlo's best hotel.

"It'll do," Carter said indifferently. He had been looking out the window. He turned back and smiled. "It'll be just fine. If you could telephone the casino and make my credit arrangements . . ."

"It has already been done, *monsieur*."

The bellmen had unpacked Carter's bags, and two floor maids had come in and were putting his clothes in the closets and drawers, while a third man, probably an assistant manager, was opening a bottle of champagne. It was Moët et Chandon, and a good year.

He poured Carter a glass, and moments later two room service waiters, each pushing a heavily laden cart, swept into the room and set up the brunch table.

"Do you wish us to remain to serve you?" one of them asked.

"No, that will not be necessary," Carter said. "I will manage on my own, and then I will need to get some rest for this evening." He turned to the manager. "Please see to it that I am not disturbed at least until early afternoon."

"*Bien sûr, monsieur*," the man said.

Within a couple of minutes the last of the service people had finished and had left, and the manager followed them, firmly closing the double doors.

Carter had arrived in Monte Carlo with a big splash. With or without his message to Rojas, the South American would get word that Carter was here. And apparently none the worse for wear.

Rojas was arrogant enough, and felt sure enough of his

position, that he would be intrigued to the point of accepting Carter's dinner invitation, if for no other reason than curiosity.

The only unknown, in Carter's mind, was how Rojas would be reacting to the news that the three goons sent to deal with Carter were missing.

Bream's men were professionals, Carter figured, which meant that absolutely no trace of the three would be found for a very long time.

The two serving carts held an assortment of gourmet dishes, each under its own silver lid, including eggs prepared four different ways, a half-dozen kinds of meat and smoked fish, caviar, a beautiful array of fruit and cheese and four varieties of crêpes.

Carter sampled a few of the items, then fixed himself a plate and brought it out onto the small terrace overlooking the city and the Mediterranean beyond.

The opening shots had been fired in their battle, and Rojas had not gone for his bolt hole. The next salvo would come this evening at the casino.

At around two in the afternoon, Carter arose from a short nap, got dressed in a casual shirt and sport jacket, and left his room.

There was one message for him. It had come in that morning at just a little before noon, according to the desk clerk.

It was, as Carter had expected, from Rojas. But unexpectedly, it was a note inviting him aboard the yacht *Princesse Xanadu*, berthed off the central docks of the Quai Albert 1er.

The docks were a pleasant walk from his hotel, but a car would call for Carter at six and would bring him down to the yacht, where they would have cocktails. Later they would dine aboard the vessel, and if the mood struck them, Rojas wrote that they would go up to the casino for the evening.

Carter looked up. The clerk had been studying him. "Pardon me, but is there someone in the hotel who might be able to provide me with information about a certain yacht in the harbor?"

"*Oui, monsieur*. I believe I may be of some assistance," the dapper man replied.

"The *Princesse Xanadu*—what can you tell me about her? It seems I've been invited aboard for dinner this evening."

"Ah, *monsieur*—you are in for a special treat."

"You know the vessel?"

"*Mais oui, monsieur*. She is a hundred-fifty-six-foot Feadship, and this is her home port."

"Who owns her?"

"Two gentlemen from Marseille who had the sense to make Monaco her home port."

"Marseille?"

"*Oui, monsieur*."

"Businessmen, perhaps?"

The clerk shrugged. "One would assume so, *monsieur*. But one would never ask."

"Yes, of course. Thank you so much for your help."

"Not at all, Monsieur Carter."

Carter turned abruptly, bumping into a young, very attractive woman who had been standing right behind him. A bellman was just coming up with her bags. She was apparently just arriving at the hotel.

"*Excusez-moi, mademoiselle*," Carter apologized, and he stepped aside. There was something familiar about her. But he couldn't place the face.

"It *is* you," she said, smiling. She was French.

Carter looked at her, suddenly remembering. He too smiled.

"You do remember . . . ?" she said, amusement in her voice.

"London. The Ritz. I came to your room by mistake."

"Yes," she said. She held out her hand. "I am André Mallier."

"Nick Carter," Carter said, kissing her hand.

She laughed. "It is only proper to kiss the hand of a married woman. Did you know that, Monsieur Carter?"

"You're not married?"

She laughed again. "Of course not. You?"

Carter shook his head. "A strange conversation we are having, *n'est-ce pas*?"

"But we met under strange circumstances." She glanced at the desk clerk, who had been watching them. "You have my reservation?" she asked.

"*Mais oui, mademoiselle*," the clerk said.

She stepped to the desk and signed. Then she turned to the bellman. "Just take my bags up. I will do my own unpacking."

"*Oui, mademoiselle*," the bellman said.

She turned again to Carter. "And now, Monsieur Carter, I propose that you buy me a drink and tell me what brought you to London and now here to Monte Carlo."

"Only if you agree to have dinner with me this evening."

"Aboard the *Princesse Xanadu*?"

"You were eavesdropping."

"A terrible habit, I admit. But yes, I think I would like to have dinner with you this evening, although I do not know a thing about you."

"Nor I you, except that you eavesdrop and that you're beautiful—all of you."

She smiled, remembering. Carter took her arm, and they went across the ornate lobby and into the grill room with its magnificent view of the city and the harbor. They were given a table by a window, and Carter ordered a bottle of champagne, then lit a cigarette. She took it from him, and he lit another.

They didn't talk much until the champagne came. The sommelier uncorked it, poured them both a glass, and withdrew.

"To this chance meeting of two interesting people," André said, raising her glass.

Carter touched his glass to hers, and they both sipped the champagne. It was excellent. "Tell me, *mademoiselle*—"

"André," the woman interjected.

"André," Carter said. "Tell me about yourself."

"Later. First it is your turn. Who are you?"

"A gambler."

Her eyes sparkled. "Evidently a successful gambler . . ." she began. "But no, you do not depend upon gambling to live. It is a sport."

Carter shrugged.

"You gambled in London?"

"Yes."

"And now here. With any luck?"

"Some recent successes. In London and Baden-Baden."

André started to say something else, but her eyes widened in recognition. "But wait a moment. You are the one who is after the South American?"

"We have gambled together."

"Everyone was talking about it at the Ritz," she said absently. Again recognition dawned in her eyes. She smiled coyly. "A gambler, but one who leaves as little to chance as possible, I would guess."

"Which means?" Carter asked. He poured them both some more champagne.

"From what I understand, the South American is wealthy. He was staying at the Ritz, no doubt on the top floor . . . one floor above my own room."

She was a very bright woman. Carter decided he was going to have to be extremely careful around her. "Go on," he said. He found himself intrigued.

"You did not come into my room by mistake. At least not through the door. You came in from the balcony after dropping down from above. Which makes you athletic as well." She smiled again and shook her head.

"And what might that tell you?"

"I don't know," she said carefully. "You are something more than a gambler. It will come to me in time."

Carter had to laugh out loud. "I believe it will come to you sooner or later. I am happy that I am not a criminal and you the police officer."

"Do not be so sure about me, Nick. I am not about you."

Carter sipped his wine. "Your turn."

"I'm from Nancy. My father, before his untimely death in an automobile accident, was a very successful attorney. And now I have a professional escort service."

Carter sat back and looked at her. "You attended finishing school somewhere, and perhaps a year or two of college."

"Finishing school in Berne. A year at the Sorbonne. But I have been a voracious reader all of my life."

"Evidently you are successful with your business?"

"My father left me a lot of money, as well as international connections. I operate my service in two dozen countries. I have more than fifty men and women in my employ."

"And yourself, André? Are you merely the administrator for this international company?"

"No," she said. "But for the moment I am on vacation."

Carter sat forward and lowered his voice. ''Then let me tell you that tonight's meeting with the South American may be dangerous.''

She smiled and raised her glass. ''What time will you be calling for me?''

TEN

A long black Cadillac limousine pulled up in front of the Hôtel de Paris, and one of Rojas's goons jumped out of the passenger side of the front seat to open the door for Carter. He stopped in his tracks when he saw that Carter wasn't alone.

"Permit me to introduce Mademoiselle Mallier," Carter said.

The gorilla, wearing a tuxedo, recovered nicely. He nodded and smiled slightly. *"Mademoiselle."* He opened the rear door, and André got in. Carter slid in after her. The goon got in the driver's side, and the limo slid away from the curb.

André was nothing less than stunning. She wore a backless, very low-cut black dress that contrasted beautifully with her complexion. Her dark hair was done up in the back, revealing her long neck. Very tiny gold and diamond earrings, a thin gold necklace, and a small diamond bracelet completed the outfit.

There would be no one at the gathering tonight, including Rojas, who would be able to keep his eyes off her.

It was a dangerous game he was playing, Carter knew, using her to run interference, but her presence would serve to push the Brazilian even further off-balance.

There was another possibility as well, Carter thought.

André's presence could very well be the stimulus needed to break Carmella Perez away from Rojas. And that woman could very well be the key that unlocked all of the man's secrets.

"Will you be like this all evening, Nick?" André asked, breaking Carter out of his thoughts.

"There may be a moment or two when I am preoccupied. I hope you will understand."

"We'll be going back to the casino later this evening, I assume."

"Probably. But in the meantime the evening may prove to be very interesting. Our host, Senhor Juan Rojas of Rio, is a very influential and strong-willed man. He will be very attentive to you."

"Is he really as rich as they say he is?"

Carter shrugged. He knew that Rojas's goon up front was listening to every word they said. "He may be."

"A strange answer."

"It's rumored that he's lost most of his money."

"Lost it? How? Gambling?"

Carter laughed. "No, I don't believe so, although he's a lousy gambler."

It took only a few minutes to get down to the docks, and they pulled up onto the central pier leading out to the individual boats. The *Princesse Xanadu* was tied up, stern to, at the outermost dock.

The evening was very warm, the breeze light, the city behind them almost blood red, the setting sun reflecting off tens of thousands of windows.

A small orchestra had been set up on the dock beside the ship, and dozens of well-dressed people were aboard sipping cocktails, laughing, and talking. A few had already begun dancing on the dock.

It looked as if many of the guests had been partying all day.

Carter and André sauntered aboard the yacht, where they got champagne cocktails and began introducing themselves to the other guests, many of whom were habitués of the gambling circuit. Most looked up in surprise, some awe, and just a little apprehension when they realized Carter was the one who had twice beaten their host at cards, the second time very badly.

For a long time Rojas was nowhere to be seen, although his bodyguards and two of the women who traveled with him were very much in evidence.

The ship was beautiful with her gently flaring bow, broad, swept-back bridge deck, huge, expensively decorated main saloon, and wide afterdeck where the bar and buffet had been set up.

Dinner, Carter suspected, would be served at midnight in the South American tradition. Either that or they'd all be Rojas's guests for dinner at the casino later. Already it was proving to be an interesting evening.

Rojas's men had evidently been ordered to keep Carter not only under strict surveillance, but surrounded as well, in case he tried something. By seven there were fully sixty people on and off the boat, among them at least a dozen of Rojas's guards.

And they had not been expecting Carter to show up with a woman in tow. Especially not a beautiful woman who turned every head in the place.

It was a few minutes after seven. Carter and André were dancing in one corner of the afterdeck along with a few other couples, when Rojas and Carmella came up from below.

Carmella was holding herself very rigid, but Rojas seemed to be in great spirits as they worked their way from the saloon out across the afterdeck, greeting people, shaking hands, having brief conversations.

Carter and André stopped dancing when Rojas and Carmella finally reached them.

"Good evening, Mr. Carter," Rojas said pleasantly. "I was surprised and, I must admit, intrigued when I got your note that you'd arrived this morning."

Carter inclined his head. "Permit me to introduce Mademoiselle André Mallier."

"I am delighted to meet you, my dear," Rojas said, kissing her hand.

"And I you, Senhor Rojas," André said.

"Please, we are all friends here. Call me Juan."

"Juan," André said.

Rojas introduced Carmella, and the two women barely acknowledged each other's presence.

"But I believe the name Mallier is familiar to me. You are not from Nancy?"

Something flashed in André's eyes. "Yes. Originally."

"Then I knew your father, Henri. His accident was a terrible tragedy. It still must hurt after all these years."

"You knew my father?"

"Yes, of course. We had some business dealings when Citröen tried to take over one of my mining operations."

"Were they successful?" Carter asked.

Rojas looked at him, the venom in his eyes barely concealed by his thin smile. "No, they were not."

"But that was another time."

"Yes," Rojas said. "Would you care to dance?" he asked, turning again to André.

"Of course, Juan," she said smoothly, and he led her to the far side of the afterdeck, leaving Carmella alone with Carter.

"I cannot believe you are actually here," Carmella said softly.

A waiter bearing a tray of cocktails came by. Carter gave

him his nearly empty glass and snagged two others, one of which he handed to Carmella.

"I told you I'd see you again."

"He will kill you! This time for sure! Don't be a fool!"

"I'm not being a fool this evening, but I certainly was most recently."

She just looked at him.

"One can never be too sure of whom one goes to bed with, can one?"

She fumed for a moment, then she reached out to slap him in the face but thought better of it and lowered her hand. Her cheeks were flushed. The action had not gone unnoticed. A number of people on the afterdeck were looking their way.

Carter took her drink from her and set it, along with his, on the aft rail. Then he led her to the ramp, down to the dock, and took her into his arms and danced her into the couples in front of the small orchestra.

She was shivering. "He is so angry, Nick. He will kill you. He has a lot of his people here."

"Why did you set me up?"

"I told you!" she snapped.

"Why don't you leave him?"

Carmella laughed bitterly. "Let's change the subject. Why have you brought a prostitute here with you?"

"Is it that obvious?"

"Yes, she is. But Juan is taken with her."

"That's why I brought her here."

Carmella looked up at him, her eyes narrowing. "What are you trying to do? Who are you?"

"I am a gambler. Nothing more."

"But why are you after Juan? There are plenty of others more vulnerable, less dangerous, around."

"Such as the Arabs?"

"Yes."

Carter shrugged. "They are no challenge. I'll let men like Juan go after them. Evidently he's in great need of ready cash. I'm surprised; I had thought he was loaded."

"He was, but . . ." Carmella began, but she cut herself off.

"I see," Carter said. "He sent you out here to get me off his back."

This time when she stepped away and swung, she did not hold back, the palm of her right hand connecting sharply with Carter's cheek.

He just stood there without flinching, without in any way reacting. A moment later she backed off, turned, and hurried back aboard the yacht, disappearing below, through the saloon, presumably to her own quarters.

Rojas and André were still dancing on the afterdeck, so Carter went back aboard the vessel, ate some of the canapés from the buffet, and had the barman pour him a stiff measure of cognac.

He leaned up against the rail, lit a cigarette, and sipped his drink.

The dancers swirled past, seemingly oblivious to him, but Rojas's goons never let down their guard. They were stationed strategically around the afterdeck, up on the bridge deck, and even on the dock itself. Every time he made the slightest move, they stiffened, ready at the slightest provocation to charge down on him.

His cheek was hot where Carmella had slapped him. Her reaction to his pressure had only served to heighten the mystery that surrounded her in his mind. Was she loyal to Rojas, as his goons were, or wasn't she? It was still impossible for Carter to tell.

The music ended, and André and Rojas wandered over to where Carter stood against the rail. They were both flushed, as if they were teenagers at a high school prom. Carter's already high estimation of André's abilities rose another notch. *Rojas may be a jerk, but he's a worldly jerk,* Carter thought. And he seemed to be falling for André.

"You looked as if you were having fun," Carter said, an edge of sarcasm in his voice.

"Juan dances beautifully," André said.

Rojas was looking around the afterdeck. "Where has Carmella gotten herself to?"

"I believe she went below to her quarters," Carter said. "We had a tiff. I think she might be jealous."

Rojas's left eyebrow rose, but before he could say anything, Carter pushed away from the rail and set down his drink.

"Thank you for the drinks and your hospitality, Senhor Rojas. Also thank your Marseille friends who own this boat. I believe I will head over to the casino. Perhaps you will join me later?"

André smiled demurely. "Yes, Juan, thank you. I hope to see you at the casino this evening."

Rojas was flustered, but there was little he could do in front of all these people.

Carter took André's arm, stepped around Rojas, and left the ship. A couple of Rojas's men fell in behind, following them up to where the cars were parked.

One of them climbed behind the wheel of the Cadillac limo, while the other held the rear door open.

Carter and André climbed in, and minutes later they were being deposited in front of the casino.

It was very early yet, so there were very few cars or people outside, nor was there much action inside. They presented themselves to the maître d' at the restaurant, who seated them instantly once he realized who Carter was. Word had spread very fast along the gambling circuit.

When they were settled with their drinks, Carter lit them both a cigarette.

"Senhor Rojas has no love for you, Nick," André said. "What have you done to the poor man?"

"Gambled with him."

"And won. Did you cheat?"

Carter chuckled. "Only insofar as I played with a very unlucky gambler."

André looked at him for a long moment. "What is it about you? Why Rojas?"

"I've already explained that one. He's an interesting challenge. Besides, I don't think I like him very much."

Again André paused. "Why is it I don't completely believe what you are telling me, and yet I feel I can trust you?"

Again Carter chuckled. "You are a very mixed-up lady. But tell me what you and Rojas talked about while you danced."

"Only if you will tell me why Carmella Perez slapped you."

"She is jealous."

"Of you and me?"

Carter shrugged.

"Delicious," André said softly. "She is Rojas's mistress. It must make him nearly insane knowing the two of you have slept together."

Carter grinned. "Is it that obvious?"

"Acquaintances don't have tiffs," she said, repeating what Carter had told Rojas. "But beyond that . . . yes, it's obvious."

"Rojas had set it up."

"To spy on you?"

Carter nodded.

"Only it backfired. She fell for you, and he knows it."

Carter said nothing, but he was satisfied that she had come to the same conclusion he had.

"One more blow against the man. It is a wonder he has not had you killed."

"He's tried."

André sat back. "I see," she said.

"I told you this might be a bit dangerous. Not directly for you, of course. But you might get caught in the line of fire."

"I'm a big girl. I can take care of myself," she said, looking at Carter appraisingly.

"I'm going to push him hard tonight. He won't like it."

"There is something else . . . another reason other than money . . . other than the macho thrill of it."

Their waiter came, and Carter busied himself ordering for both of them: escargots, a light consommé, filet of sole, and small salads.

After the waiter had left she tried again, but Carter cut her off.

"You are a wonderful woman, André, from what I know of you. But after tonight I will probably never see you again. It certainly would be too dangerous for you to be around me afterward."

"I can remain here at the casino with you until you are finished and then return to my hotel, or I can return to my hotel at this moment. Alone."

Carter just looked at her and smiled.

She returned the smile. "I think I will remain to catch at least the opening acts."

It was well after ten by the time Rojas and his party of nearly one hundred guests arrived at the casino for dinner, and nearly one in the morning before they were finished and had wandered into the gaming rooms.

André and Carter had played roulette, coming out more or less even by the time they decided to move on to something else. But by then Rojas had shown up.

He and Carmella appeared in the doorway from the grand entrance, and they stopped to survey the room. Carter and André were well across the room, a few steps from the roulette wheel at which they had been playing.

"He looks confident for a man who has been beaten, and who will probably be beaten again this morning," André said.

She was right. Rojas seemed different. More self-assured than at Baden-Baden.

Rojas hadn't looked their way yet. Carter took André's arm and quickly guided her around the fairly large group on the far side of the roulette table. He could just see Rojas and Carmella through the crowd as they moved across to the baccarat tables.

The room manager greeted Rojas, and they shook hands, said a few words, and then the manager kissed Carmella's hand.

Meanwhile, a young-looking man with a fairly dark complexion had entered the baccarat area. He set something down on the table. At first Carter could not tell what it was, but then he suddenly realized the man had brought the cards. When he turned back to leave, Carter got a very good look at him. He was definitely Hispanic. And, as in London, Carter would have bet his last franc that he was Cuban. A Cuban dealer at the Alhambra and now one here. Rojas was hedging his bets. The man had never intended on really gambling. He had intended to run the gambling circuit collecting money. A lot of money.

"What is it, Nick?" André asked.

"Rojas has had the baccarat cards rigged. They're set in a certain order. He'll get the bank, and it'll be his deal."

"You can't win!"

Carter smiled at her. "Oh yes, I can."

"Against a rigged deck?"

"A deck rigged for baccarat and nothing else. Besides, I'm nothing more than a crude American who is a little drunk. And his date is more than a little disgusted with him because of it."

A waiter came by with champagne cocktails. Carter grabbed one, spilled a little of it on the front of his tuxedo, and then, with André in tow, he weaved his way through the crowd and across the room to the baccarat table.

Rojas's eyes widened slightly when he turned and spotted Carter. They widened even further when he realized what condition Carter was apparently in. André acted thoroughly disgusted.

"Mr. Carter," Rojas said expansively. "Perhaps your luck will change this evening." He held out his hand, but Carter waved it aside, slopping some of his drink on his trousers.

The manager just shook his head and left.

"Don't need luck to beat you," Carter said. He looked at André and grinned. "Don't even need skill."

"We'll see," Rojas said. "But tonight it will be just you and me."

"Simple," Carter said, and they entered the baccarat area and took their places.

The manager returned and stood off to one end of the table to act as croupier and the club's *observateur*.

"Gentlemen, the game is—" the manager began, but Carter rudely cut him off.

"Just you and me, Rojas, right?"

Rojas nodded.

"Simple, right?"

"That's right, Mr. Carter. Shall we proceed?"

"Sure," Carter said, grinning. He held out his hand to the

manager. "Gimme a deck of cards. The bottom pack will do."

"*Monsieur?*" the manager sputtered.

A crowd of people had gathered beyond the ropes. Rojas nodded to the manager, who plucked a deck from the bottom of a stack of six decks the young man had brought over.

Carter opened it, and set the deck facedown on the table between Rojas and himself. "First I want to cut the cards."

"But they are machine-shuffled and sealed at the factory, *senhor*," Rojas said, misunderstanding Carter's intention.

"I want to cut the cards. Let's say for a million."

"*Monsieur . . .*" the manager began.

"A million francs?" Rojas asked.

"Dollars."

The crowd gasped.

Rojas shrugged. He reached out, picked up a portion of the deck, and held up a queen of hearts.

Carter smiled, picked up another section of the deck, and held up a seven of clubs.

The crowd sighed.

Rojas grinned.

"Double this time," Carter snapped.

"But we came to play baccarat . . ." Rojas protested.

"Double the bet," Carter snarled, his voice rising.

The boorish American's behavior was making everyone uncomfortable.

"Two million dollars?" Rojas asked.

"Yes," Carter said. He and Rojas replaced their sections of the deck.

"Go," Carter said.

Rojas picked up a section. This time he turned up a king. He grinned.

Carter picked off the top card and turned it over. It was an ace. He slammed it down on the table. "I win," he growled.

"Fine, *senhor*, you win. You are now one million dollars ahead. A wonderful beginning. Now shall we play baccarat?"

Carter lunged forward and grabbed the top deck of cards from the stack. There was pandemonium for a few moments. But then the crowd settled down, and Carter opened the deck.

"I don't believe I will be playing baccarat this evening," he said, all traces of his drunkenness suddenly gone.

"Your behavior is unconscionable, *monsieur*," the manager said.

"May I suggest—for the good of this establishment—that you clear the area around this table of spectators. I *most* respectfully request that."

The manager hesitated for a moment, but then he motioned for the casino security people, who had unobtrusively appeared, to do as the American requested. Rojas looked definitely uncomfortable.

When the crowd had been moved away out of earshot, the manager puffed himself up. "And now, Monsieur Carter, if you will kindly explain your extraordinary behavior . . ."

"Certainly. I will be asking for a full investigation." He dealt out the first three cards, face up. "The discards," he said. "A king, a three, and a nine." He dealt the next four cards, the banker coming up with a natural nine and the player—which would have been Carter—coming up with a seven. "The player loses that hand," Carter said. Again he dealt out two hands. This time the dealer came up with a natural eight, the player losing with a six. "The player loses again."

He dealt out a third hand, slowly placing the cards up. This time the dealer had to opt for a third card, which again put him at nine, a winner.

"What do you suppose the chances are of that happening?" Carter asked.

The manager was stunned; he could say nothing. Rojas looked as if he wanted to explode out of his chair and physically attack Carter.

Carter stood up. "I would suggest a full investigation here. Beginning with the young man who brought the cards to the table. I, for one, shall not return to this casino until I am assured personally by the Grimaldi family that such a thing shall never happen again."

He turned and strode out of the club, André on his arm.

ELEVEN

It was just four o'clock when Carter crept off the Quai Antoine 1er along the small boat docks in La Condamine. Several hundred yards across the harbor, the *Princesse Xanadu* was still berthed at the dock. Only a few of the ship's lights remained on. The band had left an hour ago, and as far as Carter could tell from where he stood, most if not all of the guests had already departed.

André had been strangely subdued after they had left the casino. Carter hadn't stopped to think about it then, but now it came to him that she had been very distant.

They had hurried out of the casino and had made their way across the Place du Casino on foot to the hotel.

Carter rode up in the elevator with her and walked her to her suite, but he did not go in.

"So you have won a million dollars," she said at her door. "Not a bad night's work."

Carter grinned. "I don't think I made him very happy."

"No," she said. There was something in her eyes that Carter missed at that moment. He was too preoccupied just then with pursuing Rojas.

But now, standing in the darkness on the docks across the

135

harbor from the *Princesse Xanadu*, it came to him that she had been holding something back.

He shook his head. Lights in the forward portholes of the yacht went out. Someone going to bed, he thought. Rojas had returned to the ship twenty minutes ago, along with some of his entourage. Since then the dock had been quiet.

A small gray Peugeot pulled up at the end of the dock's parking area. Its lights were doused, and two men got out.

Carter moved back into the deeper shadows as he watched the two men walk—no, march—down the central ramp, across the dock, and onto the *Princesse Xanadu*.

"Bingo," Carter said half under his breath. Soldiers. Their bearing and gait were unmistakable. It was what had been vaguely familiar to him about the pair at the estate outside Barnet. Those two had once been soldiers. Mercenaries?

There were many yachts berthed at the docks on which Carter had come out. A number of them had their dinghies in the water, tied up behind them. There were no lights showing on any of the boats. Either everyone was sleeping, or there were no people aboard.

Within a couple of minutes, Carter found a small Fiberglas dinghy with oars. He climbed down off the dock into the tiny boat, slipped its painter, and began quietly rowing out around the end of the dock, going straight across the harbor to the *Princesse Xanadu*.

There was a slight swell in the harbor, but it did not interfere with his rowing. By keeping well away from the shore installations to his left and the breakwater lights on his right, he could stay in relative darkness. Unless someone flashed a spotlight out there, Carter doubted if anyone could see him.

He was sweating lightly by the time he made it across the harbor, and he stopped beneath the overhang of the stern. He had so positioned himself between the ship and the dock that the only way in which he could be spotted would be if someone on the dock leaned over and looked straight down. And that person would have to know someone had come, and then they'd have to be searching for him.

For a long time Carter just sat there listening to the various sounds of the city drifting down to him, to the gentle lapping of the water against the hulls of the yachts, and to the soft thrumming of the *Princesse Xanadu*'s generators, which he suspected never slept.

Then he heard voices raised in argument. The words were faint and indistinct. But the men's voices had definitely come from aboard, and they definitely were arguing.

Rojas? Carter wondered. Arguing with the two men who had come aboard a few minutes ago?

Carter shoved the dinghy against the pilings, then scrambled up on the dock. Crouching low behind the pilings and the electric service boxes, he studied the yacht for several minutes.

There were red lights shining from the bridge, but from what he could see, there was no one up there. The crew would all be asleep. Nor was there anyone to be seen in the saloon, because the drapes over the aft sliding doors had been drawn. But up here on the dock, the angry voices were much clearer, much more distinct. Whoever was doing the talking was definitely in the saloon. Carter was certain of it.

There was no one on the docks at that hour of the morning, although an occasional car or truck passed above on the Boulevard Prince Ranier.

Keeping low, Carter worked his way around the pilings to the gangplank and scurried aboard the yacht, pulling up short just beside the saloon doors.

"We have come very far together," Rojas was saying in French.

"*Oui*," a man shouted. "And my people wish us to continue. But it takes money. Until then our hands are tied. You must understand."

"You will have your money!" Rojas shouted. "Now get out of here!"

There was a long silence. Carter was ready to move away the instant someone touched the doors, but he didn't want to miss whatever would be said next. Often in anger people revealed more than they wanted to.

"What about London?" one of the Frenchmen asked.

"What about them?"

"We understand they were paid, as were the Germans. What about us?"

"Not here," Rojas said, lowering his voice.

There was a little laughter. "Yes, we heard of your trouble at the casino. Most unfortunate."

"We go to Las Vegas next. You will be paid there."

"What about the Americans?"

"They are none of your business—for now. That will come later. For now you must be patient. All this will be ready soon, very soon. Afterward there will be more money and more power than you have ever dreamed of . . ."

Something very hard crashed into the back of Carter's head, causing the night to explode into a trillion bright lights.

His forehead banged against the doorframe, and he could feel his legs giving way beneath him.

The door slid open, and someone was talking, urgently, but the words seemed jumbled. Someone was picking him off the deck, and he was dumped onto a carpeted floor. Hands went through his pockets.

Slowly he began to come around, and he understood what had happened. He had been so intent on hearing what was being said in the saloon that he had been caught from behind.

He was in the saloon now. There was a dim light across from the long coffee table near him. Rojas stood to one side talking with two of his bodyguards and two uniformed men who were probably crew aboard the boat.

A third crewman came into the saloon. The others turned to him.

"I found his dinghy below the stern."

Rojas nodded and glanced over at Carter. His eyes narrowed.

"So, Mr. Carter, you have come to visit," the Brazilian said. He stepped away from the others and came over.

Carter had to move his head to look up. He spotted Carmella seated behind him on one of the easy chairs. She had been crying.

Rojas kicked out, the toe of his pointed shoe catching Carter in the ribs. An excruciatingly sharp pain exploded in Carter's side.

"We have your little toys, which tells me you are more than some playboy." Rojas's words came to Carter through a mist.

Someone else had come into the saloon. Rojas turned toward the new arrival, and Carter looked back, his eyes meeting Carmella's. She turned away.

"We are ready to sail, *monsieur*," the new arrival said.

"Very well. We shall leave immediately."

"For Marseille?"

"Yes," Rojas said. "But take us well out to sea before you begin angling back. There is some garbage we must dispose of, and I do not want it drifting back to litter the shoreline."

"Of course, *monsieur*," the man said.

Carmella was shaking.

Carter struggled to roll over and sit up, but Rojas shoved him back with his foot. Then he bent down so that he was very close. Carter could have reached out and killed him before his men had a chance to prevent it. But it would solve nothing.

"So," Rojas said. "You are more than a playboy. And I suspect even more than a very well-armed gambler. Just who are you?"

"I work for the CIA," Carter said. His voice seemed far away.

For just an instant, Rojas's nostrils flared. But then he smiled. "Perhaps," he said. "Perhaps not. But you do work for someone. I am sure of it."

"You're an idiot, Rojas," Carter snapped.

Rojas backhanded Carter's face. "And you are soon to be a dead man."

Carter looked up. He smiled. "How many cops do you know who tour the gambling circuit, you damned fool? I could have had you arrested for cheating in the casino. In fact, I'm surprised they didn't arrest you."

Rojas looked at him for a long time, a thoughtful expression in his eyes.

The ship's engines came to life. Carter could feel the deep-throated vibration through the deck.

"You're hiring mercenaries. How about me?"

Rojas smiled. "You want to come to work for me?"

"Sure."

Rojas laughed out loud. So did the others. The South American stood up and shook his head. "You got in my way. I do not like that. If for no other reason than that, Mr. Carter, my mysterious adversary, I would have you killed. But there is another reason you will die in an hour or so. It is because I do not trust you."

There was some activity on deck, and moments later they began to move, the ship's engines rising in pitch.

Rojas had turned back to his bodyguards. "Wait until we

are well out to sea, then toss him overboard. But first give him back his weapons and his wallet. If his body is found, I want it intact.''

"*Sim, senhor,*" one of them said.

"Have Carlos get the helicopter ready. As soon as we are clear of the harbor, I will be flying on ahead."

"*Sim, senhor.*"

Rojas turned back. "You may stay with the boat," he said to Carmella. "You can come along later with the other girls." He looked down at Carter. "Good-bye, Mr. Carter. We will not be seeing one another again."

"You're going to allow all that money I won go to my heirs?" Carter asked.

"It is of no consequence," Rojas said after a slight hesitation. "I am looking to the future." He turned on his heel and went out on deck, firmly shutting the doors behind him.

The crew had left, and now Carmella got up, looked down at Carter, and went below, leaving only Rojas's two goons.

Carter took several deep breaths to clear his head as he mentally examined his body. He was sure a couple of ribs were broken where Rojas had kicked him. But aside from those, and the lump on the back of his head, he wasn't in terribly bad condition, although his vision seemed to want to fade in and out. It was probably a mild concussion.

He looked over at the bodyguards. They were sitting at the bar, watching him.

"May I sit up and have a cigarette?" Carter asked.

One of them started to say no, but the other overrode him. "You might as well. It will be your last."

Carter sat up.

The bodyguard got off his barstool and came over. "We have your weapons, smart boy. But if you try anything, anything at all, I will work you over so that you will beg me to kill you. Do you understand?"

Carter nodded. He leaned back against the easy chair. The bodyguard lit a cigarette and handed it to Carter. Then he went back to the bar and sat down.

The yacht rose to meet the incoming swells as they sped up. Carter closed his eyes as the first couple of drags on the cigarette made him dizzy, but then his head cleared.

Forty-five minutes out, the helicopter lashed to the foredeck started up, and a few minutes later it took off with Rojas.

One of the bodyguards watching Carter went out onto the afterdeck. Carter figured if he was going to have any chance of getting out of this, it would have to be now.

"Can I have another cigarette?" he asked the lone bodyguard. He was going to have to get the man closer to him.

The guy just looked at him. Then he pulled out his pistol, a .357 magnum, and shook his head. "Not a chance."

"Big brave soldier afraid of me?" Carter snapped, trying to goad the man.

The saloon door slid open, and the other bodyguard stepped back in. "We are ready," he said.

Carter got shakily to his feet, as if he could barely stand. He wasn't faking it by much.

"We can do this the easy way or the very hard way. It is your choice," the goon holding the gun said. He was grinning, but there was a wary look in his eyes.

"Let us not play games any longer," the other gorilla said. In four steps he was across to where Carter stood, and without warning he slammed his fist into Carter's nose.

Carter's head snapped back, and he felt himself bouncing off the easy chair and crumpling to the floor. His heart was hammering nearly out of his chest. This was it! Yet he could not seem to make his arms or legs move. His head was spinning, and the light seemed to be flickering on and off.

They were doing something to his jacket and trousers.

Slowly, through the haze that threatened to totally envelop him, Carter realized they were giving him his weapons, his wallet, and the other things they had taken from him.

He had his weapons now, but he could still not move to reach them.

He was roughly hauled to his feet, then dragged across the saloon and out onto the afterdeck.

It was cool, the wind was very strong, and he could smell the diesel fumes from the engines.

They were running at full speed. He tried to make his brain work. They might be going at twenty knots. By now they'd be a long way offshore, too far to swim even for a strong swimmer in peak condition. And in these waters, which offshore were extremely cold, one might last a couple of hours—at best—before succumbing to hypothermia.

Just a little more time. The thought screamed through his brain. His head was still spinning.

He could feel himself being lifted up, and then he could see that he was hanging over the rail, the water churning in their wake.

"No!" he shouted as the two goons tossed him overboard.

He had just a moment to take a deep breath and brace himself for the tremendous shock of hitting the cold water at the speed they were going, and then he hit like an express train meeting a stone wall. He was tumbling head over heels, his battered body being hammered even more as the turbulent wake of the boat shoved him far beneath the surface.

Fighting against the tremendous pressure, against the churning water, and against his own injuries, Carter clawed his way toward the surface. He was working purely by instinct now. His lungs screamed for oxygen, and as a wounded animal fights for its survival, he understood that he could not give up.

And then his head broke the surface of the water, and he

was taking huge gulps of air into his burning lungs, his muscles cramping, his ribs sharply painful, and his head throbbing . . . but he was alive!

Gradually his vision cleared, and as he rose up on a swell, he spotted a tiny light on the horizon. The next time he rose up, the light was gone. It had been the yacht.

Slowly, each time he rose up, he scanned the horizon, one quadrant at a time. But there were no lights, and the horizon was an indistinct black blur against the dark sky.

For a while Carter relaxed, willing his muscles to go slack, willing himself to conserve his energy, but then he began to shiver, the cold water already beginning to work on him.

It would be light soon, he told himself. The sun would provide a little warmth. There would be pleasure boats. Fishermen. If that happened, he told himself, he would fire his Luger at a passing boat to catch its crew's attention. There was a chance he would be spotted.

If he could last that long.

He hunched forward, bringing his knees up around his chest in an effort to conserve body heat, but in that position he could not keep his head up. Again he had to stretch out, and again he was struck with an attack of violent shivering.

A wave of nausea came over him, and within seconds he was violently sick, his stomach emptying. When he was finished, he was weaker than before and even colder.

He was not going to make it. He began to understand that, and he began to sense that the easiest way out for him would be to simply allow himself to sink beneath the surface, and then take a deep breath. He could also use Hugo or Wilhelmina. . . .

But something within him would not allow that. Some inner drive, or animal instinct, would never allow him to give in, to hasten his own destruction.

After a while he began seeing flashes of light in the water.

But when he blinked, the lights were gone. He also began to hear an irritating buzzing noise.

He roused himself enough to look up and shake his head, but the noise persisted and became even louder.

It was a noise . . . much like a motorboat. It took a long time for that idea to penetrate. A motorboat. . . .

He looked up, sputtering. A motorboat! The sound had been much louder. Was it fading?

"Hey!" he shouted, but his voice was weak.

Quickly he fumbled in his jacket pocket. Miraculously, his penlight was still there. He pulled it out, nearly dropping it as he tried to work the switch with numb fingers.

"Hey!" he shouted again, louder this time.

The sound had died. But the penlight came on, and he raised it over his head as far out of the water as he could and swung it around, even though he felt it was in vain. The motorboat was gone.

"Hey!" he shouted in desperation. "Hey!"

"Nick?" A faint voice came out of the darkness.

He was hearing things. He swung the light nevertheless. He could not give up.

"Nick?" a woman called out. He knew the voice. . . .

"Here!" he shouted. "Here! Here!"

Minutes or hours later—he had lost all sense of time— Carter felt a line being tied around his waist, and Carmella Perez was hauling him aboard some kind of an inboard launch.

On its stern were the words PRINCESSE XANADU.

TWELVE

Within moments after he had been hauled aboard the *Princesse Xanadu*'s tender, Carter vomited again. This time he had nothing in his stomach, so he only had the dry heaves, little flecks of blood coming up with his spittle.

"Oh, Nick—oh, Nick," Carmella kept saying as she held his shoulders.

The boat was rolling heavily in the six-foot swells, and the wind was blowing the gas fumes back on them from the tender's slowly idling motor.

Carter had a hard time focusing on the woman, but he managed to smile. "You came back for me," he croaked. "How . . ."

"I knew they were going to throw you overboard, so I took the tender off the starboard rail when they went below."

"But how did you find me, Carmella?" Carter insisted. There was something wrong. It was as if someone was scratching at his consciousness. Someone or something was trying to tell him that this was wrong.

"I followed the ship's wake," she said. Tears were streaming down her cheeks.

Carter's vision began to come and go once more. But he was alive. He was out of the water.

A violent fit of shivering overtook him, and he began retching again.

Someone was grabbing at his shoulders, and when he looked up, Carmella had pulled him within the tender's tiny cabin, where she covered him with a blanket. Then she was gone.

Something was wrong. The thought kept running over and over in Carter's mind as the tender's motor roared into life and they headed back toward shore. Something was very wrong. She should not have been able to find him. Not with six-foot waves running and in the darkness.

But then those thoughts faded as Carter slipped into a semiconscious state where nearly everything was meaningless except for his own survival.

During the two-hour trip back, as the sun came up in the east from Italy, Carter kept seeing images of Rojas and his bodyguards. He kept seeing André Mallier, the way she looked when she danced with the South American, and the way she had looked in the nude when he had first seen her in her hotel room below Rojas's.

There was something about her, too, that didn't quite fit in Carter's mind, although he knew he was not thinking coherently. But he did know that when her image came into his mind, he became uncomfortable.

During the early dawn hours, he also kept seeing images of Carmella as she had been in bed with him. She had been very good, but during their lovemaking she had held back. There had been a reserve that he had not detected then, or if he had noticed, he had not assigned it any significance. He was slipping. It was another thought that drifted foggily through his semiconscious haze, but that vague feeling of having missed something important remained with him.

At one point, the tender seemed to rise up and nearly roll over to the right before coming down as if on a fast elevator, then the motion settled. They had made the harbor and were out of the swells of the open sea.

Much later, it seemed to Carter as if they had stopped, the tender just barely rocking as other boats passed.

For a while Carter was certain that both André and Carmella were there with him, helping him up, and helping him off the boat and into a car. But he knew that could not possibly be so, and he fell back into a deep, dreamless sleep.

The day was marvelous. Puffy white clouds drifted slowly in a bright blue sky, while a soft, pleasant breeze wafted in through an open window.

Carter awoke in stages, aware first that he was alive, and much later aware of the significance of that fact.

He was lying in a large bed, covered with a light blanket. He was nude except for his Rolex and for the tight bindings around his ribs. He felt battered, as if he had been run over by a truck.

For a while he was content to lie there, relaxed, totally at ease, free from any real pain, free from any immediate danger.

Gradually, however, the realization of what had happened to him imposed itself on his consciousness, and he came fully awake with a start.

He sat up abruptly, a sharp pain stitching his side where his ribs were taped.

"Christ," he groaned.

Shoving the blanket back, he got out of the bed. He managed to take only two steps before he stumbled and fell to his knees, a wave of dizziness coming over him.

He was just getting up as André Mallier came in. She stopped short for just a moment when she saw him, then rushed forward to help him back to the bed.

"Where are we, what are you doing here, and where is

Carmella?'' Carter asked. He refused to lie back.

"In that order?" André asked, looking down at him. She poured him a glass of water from the carafe on the night table beside the bed. He drank it, then handed the glass back. He still felt very weak.

"Yes, in that order," he said.

"We are in a villa just south of Monaco. It belongs to an old friend of my family," André said. "That also explains what I am doing here."

"No," Carter said. He was so tired. "Carmella picked me up. She had the *Princesse Xanadu*'s tender."

"Lucky for you."

"Too lucky . . ." Carter started to say, but he cut it off. "Are you and she working together?"

André laughed. "I don't know exactly what you mean by 'working together.' But no, we are not. I was on the docks looking for you when she came in. She asked for my help. She seemed very frightened."

"You were on the docks?" Carter asked, slumping back. It was very hard for him to keep his eyes open, to keep his mind focused.

André nodded. She eased him all the way back, then covered him again with the blanket. "Sleep," she said. "We will talk later."

"Where is Carmella?" Carter mumbled.

"She is here," André replied. "Why did Rojas want to have you killed?"

"Beat him . . . at gambling . . ." Carter said. His tongue was thick. It was difficult to form even the simplest words. It occurred to him that he had been drugged. It was probably in the water.

"Why are you after Rojas?" André asked. Her voice was coming from down a long, dark tunnel.

"I don't . . . like him," Carter heard himself saying. *No*

more, his brain screamed. He couldn't take any more. And his mind clicked off.

It was dark. The transition from bright daylight to night-time seemed almost instantaneous. Carter still lay in the bed. The windows were still open. Only now the breeze was pleasantly cool, and stars shone in the sky.

He was aware that he was not alone in the room. In the starlight he could see someone sitting just to the left of the window.

Somewhere in the house he could hear soft music playing, and from outside he could hear waves breaking on the rocks. He got the impression they were far above the water. If they were south of Monaco, that was probably true. A lot of the houses there were built on the cliffs overlooking the Mediter-ranean.

He raised his watch to eye level. It was a bit before midnight. That was not totally unexpected. But the date. It was the twenty-second. Monday. He had gone aboard the yacht early on the morning of the twentieth. On Saturday.

It meant that Carmella had picked him up that same morn-ing and had brought him back to shore several hours later.

It meant that he had slept all day Saturday, Saturday night, all through Sunday, and all day Monday.

Sixty hours. Rojas would already be in Las Vegas. And with his nemesis, Carter, out of the way, he was presumably winning big in the States. There would be further payoffs to the French mercenaries and to the American mercenaries as well.

There was some sort of a multinational force being created. The English, the French, the Germans, and the Americans were in on it. And the Caribbean was apparently the place.

At first Carter was disturbed that so much time had passed

with him out of action, but then he began to realize that, as it turned out, everything might work for the best.

Rojas would be convinced by now that Carter was indeed dead. Although Carmella was at large, Rojas would have no way of knowing for certain that Carter had been rescued.

After all, the chances of a woman alone in a motorboat finding someone floating in the middle of the Mediterranean at night, with six-foot seas running, were next to zero.

There was something wrong with that line of thinking.

Carter sat up.

"How do you feel?" André asked.

"Much better," Carter said.

"We were worried about you," she said. She was seated in the shadows. She had not moved. "You had hypothermia."

Carter got a brief mental image of lying between two nude women, but then the image faded, and he wasn't sure he had remembered it at all.

"Carmella didn't think we should call a doctor. Word would have gotten out. Rojas would have found out."

"What are you doing here?" Carter asked.

"I've already told you—"

"Who do you work for, André?" Carter insisted. That was what had bothered him all along about her. She was a professional. But her business wasn't the evening trade; it was investigation.

She didn't say a thing.

"Interpol?" he asked.

"Sure," she said.

"The SDECE? Do you work for French intelligence?"

"Sure. Them too," she said. She got up from her chair and came across the room to the bed, her body momentarily silhouetted by the starlight. She was nude.

She pulled back the covers and climbed into bed with Carter.

"You know," she said, "you talk too much about all the wrong subjects and too little about all the right ones. You are no professional gambler."

"I thought I did pretty well."

"You did all right," André said. Her body was incredibly soft. Her legs were long, and her back and shoulders flawless. She had let her hair down, and now it framed her lovely face in the dim light.

He drew her to him, and they kissed deeply for a long time, her body pressing against his, her breath catching in her throat. He could feel himself responding.

"Who do you work for?" she whispered. "The CIA?"

"Sure," he said, kissing her long neck.

"The National Security Agency?"

"Yup," he said, kissing her chin, then her throat, then lingering at each breast.

"Mmmm," she moaned, her hips moving in a circular pattern, her tongue wetting her lips. "You are a cop of some sort," she said.

"So are you."

"No," she said, breaking away. She propped herself up on one elbow and looked down at Carter. "No, I am not a cop. But I, like you, am after Juan Rojas."

"You want him dead," Carter said. He understood now.

André nodded.

"He killed your father?"

"Yes. My father represented Citröen. It was an ordinary business offer. But Rojas and his people thought differently. They killed him. I know it."

"You tracked him to London, then here. Were you in Baden-Baden?"

"No," she said. "I had business to attend to in Paris."

Another level became clear to Carter. "You have followed in your father's footsteps. You are an attorney. You work for Citröen."

"You are very astute, Monsieur Carter. I represent Citröen as well as a number of other French business concerns. But the law is not what motivates me now."

"Rojas's death does."

"Will you stop me, policeman?" she asked. She eased down and kissed his neck, then went lower, lingering at his nipples, the sensation oddly pleasant to him.

She kicked off the blanket as she worked her way down his body, past the bandages, until she took him in her mouth, her fingertips caressing his thighs. Her mouth was warm and soft and very pleasant, her long auburn hair spread out across his legs.

For a time he just lay there, luxuriating in André's ministrations, feeling himself becoming more and more excited. Finally he reached down and drew her up to him.

For just a moment she protested, but then he was kissing her breasts, and her legs parted for his caresses.

"*Mon Dieu*, Nicholas," she breathed languorously. She was moist and ready for him.

But then she pushed herself away from him and looked into his eyes. She was smiling, her eyelids half closed.

"What is it?" Carter asked. He too was ready.

"You are a marvelous man," she said. She reached out and ran a fingertip across his lips. "I am happy at this moment."

"Because of this, or because you know you will get Rojas?"

She moistened her lips. "God, I ache for you. But it is a nice pain. Do you understand that?"

"Stay away from him, André. He will kill you."

"No," she said. "He does not know me. By the time he understands what I have come for, it will be too late for him." Her hand lingered at the bandages around his side. "Does it still hurt?"

"Listen to me—you must back away and let me handle this," Carter said.

She laughed, the sound gentle. "You have only succeeded in making him angry and nearly getting yourself killed."

"I want to know what he is up to. I don't want to merely kill him."

"Then you are a cop."

"It doesn't matter what I am."

"No, it does not," André said. She lay back, drawing him to her. "Make love to me, Nick. I do not think I can wait any longer."

He entered her, but for a time he just lay there, deep inside her, while she held him very close, hurting his damaged ribs. But he didn't mind. She felt so good, her legs very long, her skin soft, her breasts crushed against his chest.

Finally he began to move, slowly at first, in shallow little teasing strokes, her hips rising to meet his thrusts. But then they lost themselves to each other, and his thrusts were deeper, with more force, and she was moaning and laughing and murmuring to him. All the while they were making love, André's eyes were open, and she was looking up at him, her lips half parted, intense pleasure evident in her features.

"Nick . . . *mon cher* . . ." she said softly. Her mouth opened as if to scream, her eyes widened, and her entire body shuddered as she came in perfect unison with Carter, their pleasure continuing in waves for a long time afterward, leaving them both limp and drained.

For a while Carter just lay still while she caressed the back of his head and neck, and he kissed her eyes, her nose, her lips.

"It has not been like that for me for a very long time," she said at last. "Did you enjoy it?"

Carter drew away from her, but not too far. He reached down and kissed her deeply. When they parted there was a quizzical look in her eyes. "Yes," he said. "I enjoyed it very much. Perhaps too much."

"What do you mean?"

"Now I'll have to worry about you," he said. He kissed her again, and this time when they parted he got out of bed.

She sat up. There was a little smile on her lips. "You are incredible, Nick," she said.

"First I need my clothes. Then a smoke, and finally something to eat. I'm starved."

She got out of bed, her whole body stretching in contentment. "I am going to take a shower in the other bathroom. You may use this one." She pulled on her robe that had been draped across the chair. "Your clothes are here in the closet, there are cigarettes on the chest, and Carmella has fixed us something to eat. It is in the kitchen."

"Where is she?"

"Sleeping. It is late. She was very tired," André said. "She was distraught. She is frightened out of her mind about Rojas. It was a very brave thing she did for you."

Carter just nodded, and then André turned and left. For a moment he just stared at the closed door. How in hell had Carmella found him out on the open sea? It still did not make any sense.

Twenty minutes later Carter had taken a long hot shower followed by an icy cold blast that instantly cleared the last cobwebs from his head. His clothes had been cleaned and were in the closet. Even his weapons had been carefully cleaned and oiled.

When he was dressed, he lit a cigarette and went into the

other part of what turned out to be a very large house. His bedroom, along with several others, were on the ground floor. Up one flight of stairs, overlooking the cliffs that went down to the sea, were the main entrance, the living room, and the dining room. The kitchen, from where a light was shining, was to the far side of the house.

André hadn't finished dressing yet, so Carter rummaged around in the refrigerator, finding a bottle of good white wine, a light potato salad, some sliced meats, cheese, and smoked fish. A long, crusty loaf of bread and a pot of hot Dijon mustard was on the table.

He had just begun his meal when André came in. She was dressed as if for travel.

"I see you've found the snack Carmella prepared," she said, sitting down across from him.

Carter poured her a glass of wine. "Are you going somewhere?"

"Yes, I'm taking the early flight to Paris."

"I see. And then perhaps Las Vegas?"

She looked at him over the rim of her glass. "Yes, Nick, I will go to Las Vegas if that is where Rojas has gone. It is my job."

"I can have you stopped."

She smiled wanly. "You *are* a policeman."

Carter said nothing.

"As a private citizen, I don't believe you could stop me from traveling to America. Or could you?"

Carter figured he probably could. But it wouldn't do much good. From what he already knew of André, he figured she'd find a way to get there no matter what obstacles she encountered.

"Can you at least wait until I get there?"

"Why don't you come with me?"

"No," Carter said. "I have to do something with Car-

mella. She's going to have to be put in safekeeping somewhere until this is over with. If Rojas gets near her, he'll have
her killed.''

"Where will you go?''

"I have friends.''

André looked at him for a long, pregnant moment. "I'll
bet you do,'' she said.

It was nearly three by the time they had finished eating and
talking. André had already packed the overnight bag she had
brought from the hotel. Her other things would be sent along.

He kissed her good-bye at the door, then watched as she
roared off in a small Fiat convertible.

He was worried about her already.

THIRTEEN

There had been a problem about Carmella's passport. She had left it with her other things aboard the *Princesse Xanadu*, so she and Carter flew first to Paris, where they took a cab immediately to the American embassy.

The ambassador was not there, but the chargé d'affaires, after a brief call to Washington—not in Carmella's presence, of course—became very cooperative.

By noon a representative of the Brazilian embassy had come over to the American embassy, and by three he had produced a new passport for her.

"Is there any trouble for you here, Senhorita Perez?" the Brazilian representative asked.

Carmella shook her head. "No," she replied. "I merely lost my passport while traveling with Senhor Carter. He was kind enough to enlist the aid of his own embassy."

The Brazilian bowed and shook Carter's hand. "Then, *Senhor*, on behalf of my government I would like to thank you for helping one of our citizens."

After he left, the chargé d'affaires got them a staff car out to Orly, and the embassy aircraft took them across the Channel and into London's Heathrow Airport.

During the trip from Monaco to Paris, Carmella had not said much. As André had said, Carmella was definitely frightened. So frightened, in fact, that she trembled most of the way. One of the flight attendents had even inquired if she was ill.

Once they had gotten to Paris, however, she had become more like her old self. Especially in front of the representative from her own embassy.

"What are we doing in London?" she asked after they had cleared British customs and were heading across the vast terminal to the cab ranks.

"I've got to find a place to stash you, and then I'm going on to Las Vegas."

Carmella stopped dead. Her eyes were wide. "God in Heaven, you are not going to Las Vegas after Juan . . ."

"Yes, I am."

"After what he has done to you?" she screeched. Passersby looked their way.

Carter said nothing.

"When he finds out you are alive he will kill you. Make no mistake about it. And this time he will be successful."

"He'll certainly try."

Carmella just looked at him but said nothing more until they had gotten a cab and were riding into the city to the Arlanda, a small, inexpensive hotel on Longridge Road.

In Paris, Carter had arranged for the hotel, and he had also arranged for someone from their London office to keep an eye on it and on Carmella.

He still had his doubts about her because of how she had found him in the water. He had asked her about it—not pressing, just curious—but she had not been able to come up with any reasonable explanation of her abilities.

There was more than an even chance, he figured, that the

entire thing had been arranged by Rojas. She had been set out in the tender, the yacht had made a very wide circle, coming back to near where she was, and then they had tossed him overboard.

If that was the case, then Carmella would have to be watched. If she took off, they'd know she was working for Rojas. Rojas wanted to know who Carter was and for whom he was working. He'd do almost anything to get that information.

"You and Juan are very much alike, you know," she said as they sped away from the airport.

"Oh?" Carter said.

"You are both pig-headed, stubborn men with dangerous streaks," she said. She looked into his eyes. "You mean to kill him, don't you?"

"Probably."

"Why?"

Carter laughed. "What do you mean, 'Why?' Christ, he's tried to kill me at least twice. And he damned near succeeded the last time."

"But what are you after, Nick? Why did you come after him in the first place? Who do you work for?"

Bingo, Carter thought. "I'm a gambler, Carmella. He was a mark."

She shook her head in irritation. "I thought we had gotten beyond that fiction a long time ago."

"What are you talking about?"

"André is no prostitute. I know that now. Juan thinks she is convinced he killed her father. It is ridiculous, but he thinks she works for Citröen and that they are out to get him."

"What do you think?"

She looked at him shrewdly. "I think you are a policeman, Nick. André thinks that too, you know."

"A cop?"

Carmella nodded.

"And evidently I'm after Juan."

Again Carmella nodded.

"I see. That also must mean that he has done something wrong. Or else why would you think a cop would be after him?"

Carmella started to protest, realizing the corner she had backed herself into, but Carter held her off.

"Just what *has* Juan done, Carmella? Why does he need money from gambling? And why was he meeting with French mercenary soldiers aboard the yacht? And they mentioned something about British and German and even American mercenaries. Just what is he up to?"

"I do not know what you are talking about, Nick," she said. Her eyes were very wide. She was panting. "I just asked why you were so intent on coming after him. You've been acting like a cop. *You* tell *me* what you think he has done wrong."

Carter took her hands. "Listen to me, Carmella. I'm not a cop. But from what I've seen in just the last week, he's done a great many things wrong."

"Such as?"

"He's obviously cheating with his gambling. The decks were rigged in Monte Carlo. And here, at the Alhambra, that young dealer I kicked away from the table was working for Juan; I'd bet my last dollar on it." Carter smiled. "That's bad enough, but then the man tries to have me killed. If it hadn't been for you, I'd be dead right now."

She sat very still.

"You still love him, don't you?" Carter asked gently.

She opened her mouth to speak, but then she backed off, leaning her head against the seat. "Yes," she said at last, her eyes closed.

"Did he send you to spy on me?"

"No, Nick!" she protested, sitting up and staring at him. "I could not let him kill you just like that. But please do not go to Las Vegas! Nothing will stop him!"

"What is he up to, Carmella? What's he doing?"

She turned away, her clenched right hand at her mouth. "Do not go after him, Nick. Please."

They rode the rest of the way into the city in silence. At the hotel they registered separately. Their bags were being sent from the Hôtel de Paris in Monte Carlo and would arrive later that evening.

"I do not feel like eating dinner tonight, Nick," Carmella said. They were in her room, having a glass of wine. "At least not out. I will have something sent up, and then I think I will go to sleep early. I am exhausted."

"I understand," Carter said.

They kissed. When they parted she looked up into his eyes. "You are not going to leave me . . . tonight?"

Carter kissed her again. "No, but I am going to go out for a while. Maybe back to the Alhambra. I've been cooped up for too long. You'll be all right alone here?"

She nodded. "In the morning we will figure out what to do. Tonight I will try to think of some way of keeping you from going to Las Vegas."

Carter managed a smile. "Sleep well," he said. "Tomorrow we'll talk more about Juan."

Both of their rooms were on the fourth floor at the front of the hotel. It was nearly seven o'clock when Carter got back to his room. He went to the window and looked down at the street.

Across the way he spotted the AXE legman. There would be one at the back of the hotel as well, just in case Carmella decided to try to slip away.

He checked his weapons and left his room, taking the elevator down.

At the desk he left a message for Carmella saying that he would be back sometime after midnight, then he stepped outside and had the doorman hail him a cab.

He made no attempt to communicate with the legman across the street, and within a minute or so, he was in the back seat of a taxi and around the corner out of sight.

The cabby dropped him off on Old Bond Street, a few blocks from Piccadilly Circus. The weather was mild, and the area was alive with its usual assortment of strange people. Piccadilly was very much like Times Square in New York City. The dregs of the city often congregated there.

At the corner of Old Bond Street and Piccadilly itself, half a block from the Royal Academy, Carter ducked into a phone booth and telephoned British Airways reservations, booking a first class seat on the Concorde SST flight to Washington first thing in the morning, with connections to Las Vegas. He'd be in the American gambling capital in time for lunch, a very early lunch, the reservations clerk assured him.

He went around the corner and sauntered up Piccadilly toward Soho with its porno shops, inexpensive restaurants, and private clubs. There were a lot of hookers and drug dealers working the streets that evening, but something in Carter's looks and bearing kept them from approaching him or pushing it too far if they missed the first signs.

Carter entered a small strip joint where he had a membership card from years ago.

He had to pay the cover charge, and once inside he sat down at the small, narrow bar. A very thin girl of no more than thirteen or fourteen was on the runway fumbling with the catch on her G-string.

Carter ordered a beer, the only drink they didn't water

down, and paid for it with a twenty-pound note.

"Keep it," he said to the burly bartender, who shrugged.

"Whaddaya want, mate?"

"I'm looking for Vincent Doyle. Seen him around lately?"

"You a copper?"

"Do I look like one?"

"Who knows?"

"I'm an old buddy of Vinnie's. We fought together in Chad a few years ago. I knew him from 'Nam in the early days. I owe him some money."

"Crap!" the barman swore. "No one ever owed Vinnie any money—" He stopped himself, realizing his error.

Carter grinned. "I'm not a cop. Vinnie and I really are old friends, and you're right; no one ever owed Vinnie a dime."

"Whaddaya want 'im for?"

"I'm just in town between jobs, you know. Thought I'd look him up, have a beer. This is his hangout. Or at least it used to be." Carter glanced up at the young, flat-chested girl on the tiny stage and shook his head. "Never understood it, but he always did like the young stuff."

"He's upstairs," the barman said, stuffing the twenty in his pocket. "I'll tell 'im you're 'ere."

Carter got off his barstool. "Never mind, I know the way," he said. "Give me another couple of beers."

The barman opened them, and Carter passed him ten pounds. "Keep it."

"Twenty-seven," the man said.

"Right," Carter said. He took the beers around behind the stage, then went up a narrow flight of stairs to the rooms.

The hallway was very dark and smelled of urine and unwashed bodies. There was a lot of noise from one of the rooms; it sounded as if someone were being killed. In this section of town, and in a place like this, it definitely paid to be deaf, dumb, and blind. It was healthier that way.

Doyle, whose full name was Vincent Quentin Doyle-Handyside III, had been born just south of London to a well-to-do family. Something had happened in his early school days, something he had always refused to talk about, that had made him the black sheep of his family. He joined the service at the tender age of fifteen, faking his ID card, and just managed to hit the tail end of the fighting in Europe.

He was in the middle of Korea in the British counterpart of the Rangers, and afterward he had commanded his own mercenary forces first for the French in the fifties in Vietnam and later all across Africa.

Carter had heard of him in Vietnam, and then he had worked with him on several occasions during the problems that seemed to plague the African continent during the turbulent sixties and early seventies.

Doyle had all but dropped out of active service after that, but all his old cronies kept coming back to him. Over the years he had become something of an expert at putting things together, as he called it. He could find the arms or the buyers; he could find troops or knew the trouble spots where troops were needed.

Doyle was a man whose ear was firmly to the ground. He knew everyone and everything in the business, and had become a very valuable friend to Carter, who never used him without returning the favor in one way or another.

When Carter had first figured out that Rojas was dealing with mercenaries from at least four countries, he thought immediately of Vinnie Doyle. If anyone knew what was going on, Doyle would. Even Whitehall conferred with the man from time to time. Unofficially, of course.

Twenty-seven was at the end of the corridor. Carter put his

ear to the door, but he couldn't hear much of anything, although there were the occasional sounds of someone in the room . . . fabric rustling, a cough.

He tried the door. It was unlocked. He took a deep breath and steeled himself for whatever he might find. The last time he had burst in on Doyle, the man had been tied to a chair, his body streaming with blood from a hundred tiny cuts, as four young girls, nude, faces and bodies made up with their versions of Indian warpaint, were cutting him with small knives.

"I don't know what makes me do these crazy things," he told Carter once. "I get all tanked up, and something pops into my head: 'Say, that'd be fun, wouldn't it?' I don't know. How's a person to understand everything that goes on in his own head . . . ?"

Carter pushed open the door. Doyle lay on his back on a narrow bed while two young teenaged girls were caressing him, themselves, and each other.

"Christ," Carter said.

"Who is it?" Doyle sputtered, sitting up and shoving both girls aside. "Who the fuck is it?"

"You goddamned pervert," Carter shouted. He grabbed the girls' robes and tossed them across the room. "Scram! Both of you!"

Giggling, the girls slipped on the robes and left. Doyle propped himself up on one elbow.

"Who the hell do you think you . . ." But then recognition dawned in his bleary eyes. "Jesus H. saves us. Carter?" he shouted. "Nick Carter?"

"One and the same, you bastard," Carter said. He handed the man one of the beers, then pulled over a chair and sat down next to the bed.

Doyle drank deeply of the beer, his Adam's apple rising

and falling. "What the hell are you doing down here in the slums? Don't tell me you've gone weird like the rest of us."

"Not yet, Vinnie. I came for some straight information."

Doyle laughed. He drank the rest of the beer and tossed the bottle aside. Carter handed the man the other beer. "All *right*! This is one son of a bitch who *knows*! Better believe it!"

"Juan Rojas. The name mean much to you?"

Doyle's eyes seemed to cross then uncross. He chuckled, then drank some of the beer. "Somalia. Don't know exactly what's up, but Somalia's the place."

"Africa?"

"Right-o. The Gulf of Aden. Oil country, I'd guess."

"What's he doing there?"

"Gathering troops. The eagles are flocking. Big bucks from what I hear. Slice of the action."

"What action?"

Doyle shook his head. "You know, it beats hell out of me. But something's going on over there. If I wasn't tied up, I'd be in on it. Got a slice of the small arms ammo deal. Netted me a few grand. Let me live, you know, for a month or so."

Doyle had been, at one time, the perfect specimen of a battle-hardened troop in class A physical and mental condition. Now he was nothing but a gone-to-fat slob whose body was criss-crossed with scars, some from battles, others from less noble pursuits.

Carter noticed a lot of needle tracks on the veins in his forearms. Doyle was doing drugs these days too. Carter shook his head. Doyle noticed it.

"Well, if it isn't la-di-da time! Gettin' too good for the likes of us?" Doyle finished the second beer and threw the empty bottle toward Carter, who ducked it easily. "You son of a bitch. Scare away my birds, then insult me. Insult to injury, I say—insult to injury.''

"What else, Vinnie? How long has this Somalia thing been going on?''

Doyle sat up, then leaned against the wall. "Don't know for sure. I first heard rumbles a couple of months ago. The big times started coming down a few weeks ago.''

"Big times?''

"You know, money—dollars, pounds, marks, francs—that sort of nosh. The loot started flowing just a few weeks ago. Before that it was mostly all talk. Interesting talk, mind you, but just gummin'.''

"Somalia is a big place, Vinnie. Can you be a little more specific?''

"Oh, sure,'' Doyle shouted. "Brings me two lousy, fuckin' beers, and now he wants the bloody Britannica.'' He reached back with a fist and slammed on the wall. "Hey, how about some beers here for a payin' customer?'' He pounded on the wall again.

A young girl wearing only a flimsy, see-through nightie appeared at the door. She looked to be about thirteen. "You bastard, what's all this noise?''

"Show her your cash, Nicky.''

Carter gave her fifty pounds. She almost fainted at the sight of the money. But she took it.

"Beer, luv,'' Doyle shouted. "An entire case of it. And be quick about it before I get more pissed off than I already am.''

"Somalia, Vinnie. Where are the eagles flocking?''

"A little place just inland from the gulf, from what I hear.''

"That's a big coast.''

Doyle shrugged.

"Don't get coy on me now. Not after all we've gone through.''

"You can't drink the whole bloody case yourself, you know, and it's already paid for."

"Maybe not, but I can throw it out the window."

Doyle just looked at him for a long minute. "You would too, wouldn't you, you bastard?"

"You bet I would," Carter said. His heart was breaking for the man. Doyle had never led an exemplary life. But just now it appeared as if he were at rock bottom.

"Yeah," Doyle said. "A camp about five miles inland, somewhere between Ankhor and Berbera."

"Oil," Carter said half to himself.

"You're goddamned right, my friend. Oil. Fascinating, ain't it?"

"How about their plans?"

"Not a tickle."

"I'm serious, Vinnie."

"So am I, Nicky, honest to God."

"How about their ordnance? Anything I should know about?"

"Usual small arms crap. They're going mostly Israeli this time with Uzis, but they've got a few Kalashnikovs from what I hear, although those pieces of iron are getting hard to come by just lately."

"What else?"

"Mortars, grenade launchers."

"And?"

"I wouldn't hold out on you, Nicky!"

"Sure you would. What else?" Carter snapped.

"All right, all right. Rocket launchers. SS-fives."

"Russian?"

"One and the same. Surface-to-surface."

The beer came. Doyle opened a bottle and drank it straight down, then opened another. Carter opened a beer for himself.

"What do you make of it, Vincent?"

Doyle grinned. "If it were me, and I was running the show? What would I be doing there?"

Carter nodded.

"I'd take over the goddamned country, no sweat, and there wouldn't be an oil ship coming through the gulf that didn't pay a toll. A *heavy* toll."

FOURTEEN

Carter walked the few blocks up to Oxford Circus before catching a cab back to the hotel. He had actually planned on going out to the Alhambra that evening for a little gambling, but his heart was no longer in it. Not after seeing Doyle.

There was little doubt in his mind that Doyle was correct in his assessment. Everyone had been watching Rojas, waiting for him to move in the Caribbean, while all along his intentions had been in another, totally opposite direction.

Somalia. Africa. It used to be French but had a history of British occupation. Mostly desert, some interior highlands. Always seemed to be a lot of trouble out there of one sort or another. Never could get along with her neighbors.

But that was about the extent of Carter's knowledge of the country, except that its capital city was Mogadishu, which had been an active British port at one time.

Actually, it was a beautiful setup. The Americans and the Russians were vitally interested in the area because of the oil.

Presumably Rojas was working under the Soviet imprimatur so that when the shooting began they wouldn't do much. The U.S. government would probably be too busy elsewhere to respond as quickly as would be necessary.

Once the shooting began, Carter doubted the war would last longer than twelve hours tops.

Take over the capital, the military and police barracks, the radio and television station, and the other ports, and it would be all over. As Doyle said, no sweat.

It would take two elements to accomplish that, however. The first was Rojas himself—he gave the orders—and the second would be the ordnance, especially the rockets.

Back at the hotel, the cabby dropped Carter off at the front entrance. Before he went inside, Carter glanced across the street. The legman was still there. Evidently Carmella had not moved from her room.

He was surprised. Perhaps he had been wrong about her after all. Perhaps she was just an innocent young woman who could not decide where her loyalties ended and her sense of morality and decency began.

He stopped at the desk to check for messages. There were none for him, nor had Senhorita Perez called for hers.

That was surprising too, Carter thought as he turned away. He would have thought Carmella would have been down here checking on messages, perhaps phoning out.

Another chilling thought struck him, and he went back to the desk. "Senhorita Perez," he said. "What did she have for dinner?"

"Sir?" the startled night clerk asked.

"Senhorita Perez—did she have food sent up to her room?"

"Why, no, sir. There have been no calls in or out of your rooms."

"Christ," Carter said, and he raced to the stairwell, tore open the door, and headed up the stairs, taking them two and three at a time.

She was in love with Rojas, and only recently had she come to understand exactly what he was. She had seen what he had done to Carter, and no doubt André had talked with her about what Rojas had done in France.

It all had to add up to a gigantic paradox for the mixed-up young woman. An insolvable problem.

He came to the fourth floor, flung open the door, and raced down the corridor, skidding to a stop at Carmella's room. He pounded on the door.

"Carmella!" he shouted. "Carmella!"

There was no answer. A couple of doors along the corridor opened, and heads poked out. "Someone call an ambulance. Hurry! It's an emergency!" he shouted.

He pounded on the door again, then reared back and slammed into it with his shoulder. The wooden door opened easily, the lock and chain pulling out with a pop.

Carmella was in bed, the covers pulled up to her chin. A soft light was burning in the corner, and the television was playing softly. Some British comedy.

Carter approached the bed very slowly. Carmella appeared peaceful, as if she were sleeping, but he knew better. He had seen enough dead people to understand that Carmella was not merely sleeping.

He touched his fingertips to the carotid artery in her neck, but there was no pulse. Already her flesh was cool to the touch.

On the night table was a pill bottle and half a glass of water.

Carter picked up the bottle. It was a prescription for sleeping pills from a Paris pharmacy. He opened the bottle and looked inside. He looked again at Carmella, and he noticed a slight grimace on her face. As if she may have died in some pain. Or at least felt pain while she was asleep.

The pill bottle was nearly full. She had not killed herself with an overdose.

Carter bent down over Carmella's body and sniffed her lips. There was the faintest odor of almonds. He shook out one of the capsules and opened it, pouring its contents into the palm of his hand. The odor was unmistakable. Strychnine. She had been poisoned.

He looked at her again, and the muscles in his jaw tightened. Rojas knew that all of this was upsetting her. He knew that she would begin to have trouble sleeping. The man knew that sooner or later she would take a sleeping pill to calm her nerves, to help her sleep. He had probably suggested she get them. Then he had somehow gotten them from her and had switched them with the strychnine-laced capsules. Carter could almost hear the blood singing in his veins, his muscles bunching up. *The son of a bitch*. . . .

There was a commotion out in the corridor. Carter slipped the capsules into his pocket and dropped to his knees beside Carmella.

The manager rushed in a moment later. "What is it? What is all the trouble up here? There are guests trying to sleep . . ."

The manager stopped in mid-stride. Carter turned to look up at the man.

"She is dead. My friend is dead. Her heart."

"Good Lord," the manager breathed. "I'll ring up the doctor."

"No need for him now," Carter said.

The night seemed to go on for a long time. The doctor came, then the coroner and the police, and finally her body was taken away.

There was no longer such a great need for secrecy and stealth now that Carmella was dead, so Carter made a couple of telephone calls to his people in London, and by morning he was free to go.

The cabby just got him out to Heathrow in time for his SST flight to Washington, D.C. He had coffee and very good sweet rolls in the VIP lounge, and then he was aboard the high-flying jet, the sky a deep, dark blue at the altitude they flew.

From the very beginning he had had mixed feelings about Carmella, but he had not been able to put his finger on just what it was that had bothered him. Not until this moment.

Carmella had been a woman frightened to death of her own life. She had somehow known all along that she would end up this way. It frightened her so badly that she was like a doe who suddenly found herself on a superhighway at night, the lights of a truck bearing down on her. She knew she was in mortal danger, but she was too frightened even to move out of the way.

He should have seen that. He should have helped her get away.

Carter only picked at his food during the short flight across the Atlantic, had only one drink, and rejected the attempts of the good-looking young woman seated next to him at conversation, despite her repeated efforts.

He had a half hour between flights, and David Hawk himself was waiting in the cocktail lounge just down the corridor from the Air West boarding gate where Carter was to catch his plane to Las Vegas.

Carter almost walked by the open lounge door, when he happened to spot Hawk seated at a corner table. He went in, got himself a large cognac, and sat down with his boss.

"London phoned a couple of hours ago about the girl. Said you were hit hard," Hawk said, his gravelly voice low.

It was fairly early in the morning, Carter suddenly realized, and yet the bar was open. He looked around. There was no one else there. The bartender looked familiar. An AXE employee, probably.

"It's not the Caribbean after all. Rojas is running an operation in Somalia," Carter said to Hawk.

"What sort of operation?"

Quickly and succinctly Carter explained what he had come up with so far, leaving out all but a casual reference to André Mallier. But Hawk was sharp, and he knew Carter like a father knows his son.

"You only used this Mallier woman as a smoke screen that night on the yacht and then later at the casino?"

Carter took a deep breath and let it out slowly in an effort to clear the pressure in his chest. "There's more," he said.

"I thought so."

Carter explained André's background, and then her help in the house south of Monaco.

"Do you think she is in Las Vegas now?"

Carter nodded. "Yes, I do."

"And you're going there now . . . to kill Rojas?"

Carter looked up, directly into his boss's eyes. David Hawk had the reputation of being an exceedingly tough old man. It was said his heart was made of granite, and only ice water flowed in his veins. Carter knew better. At that moment there was compassion in Hawk's eyes.

"Yes, sir," Carter said. "Afterward I'll go to Somalia."

"Do you want help?"

"I don't believe that would be wise, sir. If we go in there in force, officially, the Russians will get involved in a big way. It would be a mess."

Hawk thought for a long moment. "I agree," he said. "But one word of advice, Nick."

"Sir?"

"It wasn't your fault about the Perez woman, so don't take on the responsibility for André Mallier. You have a job to do, an important one. Don't forget that."

"I won't, sir. It will be my first priority."

Hawk's eyebrows rose, and he started to protest, but then

he just shook his head and smiled. "Good luck, Nick. If you need help, we'll be there."

Hawk got up and left the lounge. A minute later Carter finished his drink and headed over to the Air West boarding gate. The bartender came around the bar, closed the gates, and left the back way.

McCarran International Airport was busy, thousands of people coming and going, the public address system paging passengers, and all the while the ever present slot machines created a cacophony unlike anyplace else in the world.

From the Air West boarding area, Carter had managed to contact the Hôtel de Paris in Monte Carlo. He asked them to transfer his funds to Caesars Palace in Las Vegas and to reserve a suite for him there.

They had, and they had evidently sent along Carter's description too, because just outside the main doors of the airport, a uniformed chauffeur approached him.

"Mr. Carter?"

Carter turned to the man and nodded.

"Yes, sir," the man said, taking Carter's bags, "The hotel in Monte Carlo called and said to pick you up, sir."

Carter grinned. "Sure thing," he said. High rollers the world over were treated well.

He climbed into the back seat of a Rolls-Royce, and within a minute they were speeding into town.

"You're the talk of the town, Mr. Carter," the chauffeur said.

"That a fact?"

"Yes, sir. Or at least you are in certain circles, if you know what I mean."

"No, I don't. What do you mean?" Carter asked.

The driver glanced at him in the rearview mirror, guessing

that he might have gone too far. "I didn't mean no disrespect, Mr. Carter. Honest."

Carter laughed. "No sweat." He lit a cigarette. "I suppose everyone in town has heard about my little streak in Monte Carlo."

The driver whistled. "Little streak! Are you kiddin'? From what we hear, you didn't do so bad in Baden-Baden or London neither."

Again Carter laughed. "It's a living."

"I guess."

For a few minutes Carter fell silent, staring out at the desert, at the ramshackle houses and businesses on the outskirts of the town. He used to come here a lot a few years back. But it had been a while.

"Where's the action this week? Anything big?"

"We had a splash last night at Caesars. A little action upstairs. The Tropicana has the national poker thing goin' again. Slim and Amarillo and some of the other dudes are in town."

"You heard of a roller named Rojas? Juan Rojas?"

"Oh, sure. He breezed in a couple of days ago with his army. He's been makin' a buck or two around town. I think he's settin' himself up for a big win. Everyone thinks so."

Vegas may have heard about his wins in Europe, Carter thought, but it evidently hadn't heard that the big challenge had been between himself and Rojas.

"Where's he staying, at Caesars? M-G-M?"

"Nah. He's shacked up out in the desert with this goodlookin' French dish . . . André somethin' or other."

Something clutched at Carter's gut. He had a clear image of how Carmella looked lying dead in the London hotel room. He did not want a repeat with André.

"Does he come to the Strip?"

"Sure, every night. How do you think he gambles?"

"Where's he staying?" Carter asked again.

The driver looked at Carter in the mirror. "Are you after him or somethin'?"

"Who do you suppose I won all my money from in London and Baden-Baden and Monte Carlo?"

For a moment the driver said nothing, but then his face lit up. "Well, I'll be damned! From Rojas? No kiddin'?"

"No kiddin'. Now, where's he staying?"

"Oh, man, this is goin' to be great! It's a few miles outta town on the Tonopah Highway. Called Don Chavez's Place. Some Italian tycoon owns it. Comes over once in a while."

"Where does Rojas usually look for his action?"

"He's been comin' to Caesars mostly. That's how come I know so much about him. Usually comes in around midnight."

"With the woman?"

"The French gal? You bet. She's a real looker."

"I can hardly wait to meet her," Carter said, and he sat back.

Carter's suite was on the top floor of Caesars Palace. For nearly a half hour the staff of the hotel fussed over him, making sure his bar was stocked, making sure his bags were unpacked and his clothes cleaned and pressed, making sure he understood that he had an unlimited line of credit anywhere in Vegas—but especially at Caesars—and making sure that there would be no trouble. Management had heard of his feud with Rojas.

"A delicate matter, Mr. Carter, but one which I'm sure you can appreciate," the manager said just before he left.

Carter waited for him to continue.

"Mr. Rojas travels with his . . . companions. None of them are . . . armed as long as they are in our hotel. We would hope that you conduct yourself appropriately."

Carter smiled. "Of course."

"Then I shall leave you. We hope you enjoy your stay."

"I will. Believe me, I will."

"Yes, sir."

"Oh, by the way, before you go—I'll need to rent a car. Something large. Perhaps the Rolls that I was picked up in?"

"Of course. Will you need a driver?"

"Yes. In fact, I'd like the car out back right now. The driver, the one who picked me up at the airport—what's his name?"

"Ernie."

"Ernie can just stand by. I'll call him when I need him."

"Very good, sir."

After the manager left, Carter unsnapped his cassette recorder and removed his weapons. He donned his gas bomb, but he just slipped the stiletto and Luger in his jacket pocket.

He was downstairs, by the back way, just as Ernie was parking the Rolls. The chauffeur got out, then spotted Carter.

"Do you want to go someplace now, sir?"

"Not right now, Ernie. A little later tonight."

"I'll be ready anytime you are, sir."

"Good," Carter said. He turned and went back into the hotel, but then he stopped. He watched the driver putter around the car for a couple of minutes then go across the driveway and enter another part of the hotel complex.

Carter walked back outside, went over to the Rolls, and climbed into the back seat. Making sure no one was watching, he quickly stashed Wilhelmina and Hugo beneath the front seats.

Tonight, he thought, getting out of the car and going back into the hotel. Tonight he and Rojas would come face to face, and it would be for the last time.

He had a light lunch in the hotel's coffee shop, then played a few hands of blackjack at one of the tables, coming out a hundred dollars ahead.

Back up in his suite, he made sure the door was locked, then he peeled off his clothes, took a very long shower, had one quick brandy, and crawled into bed. It had been a day and a half since he had gotten any sleep. He was going to have to be well rested for tonight's action.

He fell asleep almost immediately, and he dreamed of Carmella and André. They were both in trouble. They were running down a long dark alley, pursued by a ten-foot-tall Rojas with long fangs and claws.

Carter was there, but he could never seem to get his legs going. He wanted to help, but he simply could not move, and he cried out in frustration as Carmella went down, blood everywhere.

It was dark when he awoke, bathed in sweat, his heart pounding. He looked at his watch. It was a little before ten.

Carter got out of bed, flipped on the room lights, and called down to room service. He ordered a large steak, rare, a small salad with oil and vinegar, and a bottle of Bordeaux.

While he waited for his dinner to come, he took another shower, shaved, and got dressed in his evening clothes. He felt naked, however, without Wilhelmina and Hugo.

He put on some music when he had finished dressing, and minutes later his meal came. He tipped well, then sat down and ate slowly, finishing the bottle of wine. Afterward he lit a cigarette and poured a large cognac.

He went to the window and looked down at the Strip, which never failed to impress him. There was no other place in the world like it. Monte Carlo, Baden-Baden, Deauville, and the other European gambling places, with their Old World elegance, were as quiet as tombs compared to Las Vegas.

For a few minutes, standing there, he could forget why he had come to Vegas. He could simply relax and enjoy the moment. But then he thought about his dream, which was still vivid in his mind and which brought him back to Carmella lying dead in a London hotel room, and finally to André, somewhere in the Nevada desert with Rojas.

Finishing his cognac, Carter stubbed out his cigarette, made sure he looked all right in the mirror, and left his room.

Without weapons, Rojas's goons would be relatively ineffective in the Caesars casino. Once outside, however, it would be a different story unless Carter had the advantage.

It was just approaching midnight as Carter wandered across the casino and walked to the baccarat table just across from the main bar.

Already four men in tuxedoes had gathered at the table, one of them Juan Rojas. On the far side of the railing were three of his bodyguards. Seated next to Rojas was André.

There were several other people standing around, so Carter was able to slip inside the rail without being noticed. He came around the table and stood directly across from Rojas.

André noticed him first. Her eyes went wide, and she made a little cry. Rojas turned to see what had caused her reaction. Carter was satisfied to see that for a long moment—it almost seemed like hours—the man was vexed. He knew Carter had shown up in Vegas. He had to have known it. But seeing him here now, like this, was a blow to his ego.

All hell would break loose very soon, Carter decided. Very soon indeed.

FIFTEEN

"Senhor Rojas, Mademoiselle Mallier," Carter said pleasantly. He sat down, took out his cigarettes, and lit one.

The cocktail waitress came and Carter ordered a glass of champagne.

André had averted her eyes, but Rojas was staring at him. The South American's bodyguards were straining at their leashes on the other side of the barrier. Carter found that he was almost hoping they'd make a try for him. Obviously Rojas had good control over his men.

"It's curious to see you here so soon," Carter said.

If other people at the table noticed that something was going on between Carter and Rojas, they did not show it. The cards had not yet arrived, but the game would soon begin.

"Curious in what respect, Mr. Carter?" Rojas asked, finding his voice.

"I meant so soon after Senhorita Perez's death."

André sucked in her breath and closed her eyes.

"I am sorry, Mademoiselle Mallier," Carter said. "I was certain Senhor Rojas had informed you. Poor Carmella—the French police are still looking for her murderer. She was poisoned, you know. Strychnine in her sleeping capsules. Ingenious, actually. Just as her rescue of me was ingenious."

The two men seated at the far end of the long table, who both looked like Texas oil barons in their Western-cut tuxedoes, looked first at Carter, then at Rojas.

Carter glanced over his shoulder at Rojas's three body-guards. One of them he recognized from the yacht. "And you," Carter said to him. "Before this is all over I'm going to break both your arms and legs. And that's for starters." He turned back.

The house man came with the shoe and the cards. Carter stood up, stubbing out his cigarette. His drink had just come, and he drained the glass.

"Sir?" the house man asked uncertainly.

"I won't play at this table with that man," Carter said in a loud voice. He pointed at Rojas.

The others around the table looked up at Carter.

"Sir?" the house man asked again.

"His name is Juan Rojas. He is a cheat, a liar, a thief, and a murderer. Ask him about the baccarat table in Monte Carlo. And ask him about a woman named Carmella Perez, until recently his mistress, whom he poisoned."

There was chaos. Two of the men at the table jumped up. Rojas's bodyguards tried to come over the barriers, but the house security people had materialized as if from thin air and restrained them.

Rojas remained where he was seated, a very thin smile on his bloodless lips. "You have gone too far, *senhor*," he said softly.

Carter laughed out loud. "As I said once before, Rojas, you're a fool!"

Carter turned on his heel, stepped through the gate in the barrier, and strode across the casino to the desk.

"I'm Carter. I want my driver. Now!" he snapped.

"Yes, sir," the flustered clerk said.

Carter turned and went back through the casino to the back

door. There was still a lot of commotion around the baccarat table.

He stepped outside. It was very dark. One of the overhead lights had gone out. The Rolls was parked just across the driveway. Carter hurried across to it, opened the back door, and slid inside.

Ernie was there. "Mr. Carter," he said.

"We're going to have company in just a second or two, so let's get the hell out of here," Carter said, reaching for his weapons. But they were not there.

"Looking for something?" the chauffeur asked.

Carter straightened up to look into the muzzle of his own Luger. "I see," he said.

"Sorry, but the other bozo has got more money than you. And certainly a lot more muscle."

"May I light a cigarette?" Carter asked.

"I don't care."

Carter lit a cigarette as Rojas, André, and three bodyguards came out the back door and headed straight for the Rolls.

The bodyguard from the *Princesse Xanadu* yanked open the rear door and looked in at Carter.

"You shouldn't take things so personally," Carter said.

The bodyguard reached for him, but Carter slid away.

Rojas shoved the man aside and got in the back with Carter. André was beside him at the window. One of the bodyguards opened the other door and slid onto the back seat, shoving Carter over, the two other goons piled into the front.

Ernie started the car, and they pulled away from the hotel.

"You talked bravely in there, Mr. Carter," Rojas said with an edge to his voice. "I wonder how brave you will be one hour from now?"

"Are you going to pull out my fingernails?"

Rojas chuckled. "Actually, I have something far more

civilized in mind, though no less painful.''

''What do you want, besides my money?''

''I want to know who you work for.''

''The CIA, I've already told you.''

''As much as I would like to believe that, I do not. And yet . . .'' Rojas let it trail off.

They were driving on the Strip now, heading northwest out of the city.

''Why did you kill Carmella?'' Carter asked.

Rojas said nothing.

''You bastard,'' Carter snarled. Then he switched to Portuguese and let fly with a string of the worst obscenities he could think of, most of them involving Rojas's mother.

Rojas lunged at him, and Carter just managed to swing a left hook that connected solidly with the man's jaw. Rojas's head snapped back at the same moment the bodyguard beside Carter grabbed his shoulder.

Carter rolled left this time, swinging his weight behind a right hook that slammed into the side of the big man's face. He slammed his fist into the man's face again, then a third time, before he felt the cold metal of a very large gun barrel pressed against his head.

''Another move and your brains will decorate the rear window,'' one of the bodyguards from the front seat said.

Carter forced himself to relax his muscles, to slow down, to settle back.

Ernie had slowed the car and was about to pull over to the side of the road, but Rojas ordered him to go on.

''Not here, *imbecil*!'' he shouted. ''Wait until we are out of the city. At least that far.''

''Where I will kill you,'' Carter said softly.

Rojas shoved the gun barrel aside and slapped Carter hard in the face. ''Kill *me*? Are you crazy?'' The Brazilian was nearly berserk with rage.

"We know about Somalia; we know all about it. Your little base is—"

Rojas slapped him again. "You don't know anything!"

"We know about the mercenaries: the Americans, the French, the Germans, even the British. Who do you think killed your British mercenary at the Château Le Favre outside Barnet?"

Rojas was shaking. Spittle drooled from the corners of his mouth. His bodyguards in the front seat looked uncertain now.

"The base," Carter said, "is about five miles inland between Ankhor and Berbera. Your people even have SS-fives."

"What are you talking about?" Rojas screamed.

"Once your people are finished in Mogadishu, you think you'll be able to control the oil traffic through the Gulf of Aden. But it won't work, Rojas."

Ernie had turned off on Lake Mead Boulevard, north of the city, and he swerved the car off the road to the right, laying on the brakes, the big car slewing first right and then left.

In an instant, Ernie was out of the car and racing off into the night.

The gorilla next to Carter had pulled out his pistol, but Carter snatched it out of his hand and fired two shots into the front seat, both bodyguards pitching forward.

André opened the door on her side and jumped out as the remaining bodyguard grabbed Carter's left arm and slammed it forward over the back of the front seats, causing him to drop the gun.

Rojas leaped out of the seat after André as Carter slammed his fist into the side of the bodyguard who was twisting his arm farther and farther over the front seat.

The pain suddenly became unbearable, and the bones of Carter's arm snapped with a loud pop.

The man let go at that moment, figuring the fight was over, but it was a fatal mistake. Carter, working on pure instinct, swiveled around, reached up with his right arm, and grabbed the goon's windpipe in his powerful grip. Steeling himself, Carter reared back, pulling with every ounce of his strength, and ripped the man's throat open, blood spurting everywhere.

The bodyguard lashed out, his entire body jerking in macabre spasms as he fought a losing battle for his life.

Carter held him off for a minute or so until finally the man's struggles weakened and then ended as he slumped over, dead.

In great pain now, Carter reached into the front seat and grabbed the gun from where it had fallen between the two dead bodyguards, then slid across the seat and climbed out of the car.

He took a half-dozen steps away from the car before he spotted Rojas and André.

"That's far enough!" Rojas shouted. He had André by her hair, her head pulled back, the point of a stiletto at her neck . . . Carter's stiletto.

"Let her go, Rojas! This fight is between you and me," Carter shouted, stepping a little closer. He was about twenty feet away.

"Come any closer and I will kill her," Rojas shouted.

Carter raised the big .357 magnum. "You kill her and you are a dead man. Automatic, Rojas. But I'll make a deal with you. Give you a chance."

"What kind of a deal?" Rojas shouted after a moment.

"I'll throw down my gun. You keep the knife, but let André go. It'll be a fight between you and me."

Rojas said nothing. Carter knew the man was weighing his chances.

"I'll have no weapons. My left arm is broken. You'll have a knife."

Still Rojas maintained his silence.

Carter taunted him again in Portuguese, then threw the magnum far out into the night. He held out his right hand, his left arm hanging useless at his side. "Well?" he called.

Rojas stood silently for a long time. Finally, however, he shoved André aside, sending her to her knees, and he raced forward.

It was a fool's lunge. Carter stepped aside and easily tripped the South American, sending him sprawling on his face in the dust.

Carter came at him, but before he connected, Rojas had rolled over and had sprung up in a crouch, swinging wildly with the stiletto, the point of the blade opening a large gash in Carter's side.

Carter feinted left, Rojas lunged that way, and Carter pulled back, bringing his knee up and catching Rojas in the crotch.

Rojas doubled over as he scrambled backward, dropping the stiletto on the ground.

Carter lunged for the knife, but even in pain Rojas had enough presence of mind to kick out, his formal pump catching Carter squarely in the left arm below the elbow. The pain was so excruciating that the desert sky lit up like the Fourth of July, and Carter's head spun as he reeled back.

It seemed like hours, but it was only seconds, before Carter could see anything, much less regain his balance. Rojas lay curled up in a fetal position. He was groaning and rolling around, clutching his crotch.

Carter limped forward and picked up his stiletto. Rojas was finished. There would be no fight left in him now. Carter didn't think the rest of his bodyguards would want to continue the fight with their leader down.

He had told Hawk he was coming to Las Vegas to kill Rojas. But now that the opportunity presented itself, he knew it wasn't worth it. The man was the scum of the earth, but he was beaten.

All that was left was Somalia. Someone else would have to do that now. But it would be relatively easy, he supposed. With Rojas out of the way, he did not think the mercenaries would have much interest in the fight.

Rojas sat up at last and shook his head. He looked up at Carter.

"You bastard," he said with much feeling.

"Yeah," Carter said. He started to turn to see how André was, when she raced up out of the darkness. She had the .357 that Carter had thrown away held in both hands straight in front of her.

"No!" Carter shouted.

Rojas raised his right hand as if to ward off a blow. André fired, the first shot catching him in the chest just above the breastbone.

His body was slammed backward, and her next shot went over his head into the sand. But then she was standing over his still twitching body, firing into it, the first point-blank shot taking off his face and most of the back of his head, the second destroying his neck. The next time she pulled the trigger, the hammer snapped on an empty cylinder. She kept on pulling the trigger, the hammer snapping, until she finally threw the heavy pistol at Rojas's body. It landed on what was left of his chest.

"André," Carter said.

She came to him slowly, and he encircled her with his good arm while she sobbed. In the distance Carter could hear sirens. Someone had reported the shooting.

Somalia, after all, wasn't really important. It had been

ojas. Whether his interests had been in the Caribbean or in frica, it would not have mattered. It was he who was evil. nd now he was dead.

It was time, Carter thought, to take a vacation. A very long acation.

DON'T MISS THE NEXT NEW
NICK CARTER SPY THRILLER

THE KREMLIN KILL

Strong hands lifted his shoulders and then his legs. The door opened before them, and Carter realized with a shock that night had come again.

It had been a day and a half since he had crawled into the girl's cart and made the trip up to the hacienda.

Now, somewhere out in that darkness, Farrell and Felipe Cordova would be watching him emerge. Carter hoped they would be smart enough to split themselves up.

If Carl and company got away again, it would be almost impossible to pick up the scent until they all hit Geneva.

And then it might be too late.

Carter had very little feeling in his arms and legs as he was bounced through the door and down the front steps. He tensed, relaxed, and tensed again.

It was the ties they had put on his wrists and ankles; the knots were biting right into the skin.

But then, what did his circulation matter to them? In a short amount of time, as far as they were concerned, his circulation would stop anyway.

For good.

The cool night air on his face helped revive him further before the rear door of a Cortina was opened and he was thrown headlong into the back seat. The smaller of the two, a mean-faced little man with a mustache and black, stringy hair to his shoulders, prodded Carter down from the seat to the floor.

You bastard, Carter thought, *when the time comes* you'll *be the first to go!*

The rear door slammed, jolting the bottom of Carter's feet, and the two crawled into the front.

Then they were moving. He sensed rather than saw the car pass through the gates, and then felt the angle shift as they started down the hill.

Fifteen minutes later, the lights of the village went by the window and they were again on the open road beneath a moonless black sky.

The ride seemed to go on forever, at least hours, and at a pretty reckless speed.

Every time Carter tried moving to get a little circulation back in his arms and legs, thunderbolts of pain shot through his head and throat.

"Do they follow?"

"*Sí*, with their lights off."

"Should I go slower?"

"No. We do not want them to think we are bait."

Carter thought that he could get his legs high enough to flip the door open, but he knew the move would be foolish.

If he threw himself from the car on these mountain roads at this speed, there would be little left when they did get to him.

Carter had been much closer to death than this, many

times. But each time before, he had been somewhat prepared for it.

By rights, he knew he should be feeling fear. Any man who was about to die and didn't feel fear was a damned fool. Fear made you sharper. And right now Carter knew he needed to be sharp.

But he wasn't.

He felt dulled, and more full of anger than fear.

He had blown it by being in too big a hurry. He should have waited until they were all in their rooms, asleep, and then made his move.

But he hadn't.

And now he was paying for it in a cataclysm of pain and darkness, hurtling through the night, with two very highly trained killers as his chauffeurs.

Suddenly the car screeched to a halt. Through the open front window on the driver's side, Carter could smell the sea.

Both of the men left the car at once. Carter heard them step away a few paces, and then one of them called.

"Manuel?"

"*Sí*."

"Is the boat ready?"

"*Sí*."

"And the others?"

"Christo and Garcia are up there in the rocks. They will get them."

"Good."

Dammit it to hell, Carter thought. Whoever was behind them, Farrell or Cordova—or both of them—was walking right into it.

He would have to start it himself before they got there.

He heard the footsteps return. There was deathly silence for a few seconds, and then both rear doors were yanked open at once.

The little one with the mustache started pulling Carter unceremoniously out by his bound ankles, while the other one pushed at his shoulders.

Nick's feet barely touched the ground before he fell forward in a tuck. Then he rolled, throwing his painful, blood-denied legs against the other man's.

He could barely see, but he could feel, and the feel was good. The little man went down with a plop and a grunt, with Carter right on top of him.

"Ricardo . . . the bastard is awake!"

The words had hardly left his lips as Carter lined up, head above head. Then he came down with all the force in his shoulders and neck. His forehead hit the little man's chin, bringing a sobbing groan from his throat. It had barely died out before Carter came again, this time forehead to forehead.

The man went out like an extinguished candle.

—From *The Kremlin Kill*
A New Nick Carter Spy Thriller
From Charter in October